JUDY GARLAND and the *Hoodoo Costume*

An original story featuring

JUDY GARLAND

famous Metro-Goldwyn-Mayer motion picture star as the heroine

By

KATHRYN HEISENFELT

Authorized Edition

Illustrated by

RUTH RUHMAN

WILDSIDE PRESS

CONTENTS

Judy Searched for the House Number

JUDY GARLAND
and the Hoodoo Costume

CHAPTER ONE

MESSENGER GIRL

The girl extended both her arms to balance herself as she stepped cautiously over the ice-encrusted sidewalk. At noon the December sun had held the power to reduce the smudged humps of snow to trailing rivers, but there was weariness in its fading light at this late hour. A chill wind cut through the gathering gloom, gaining mastery. It settled the ice more firmly, and woefully stirred the branches of thick, bare trees, promising an end to the spell of mild weather.

The trees which bordered the sidewalk were out of place here, but evidently the street had seen better days. There had been fine homes here, once, substantial and prosperous. Now the residential district had become a business section. Newer apartment buildings, bakeries, an upholstery shop had edged in among the ancient, square houses.

Coming to one of the old frame buildings, the girl paused, searching for the number over the door—

the number of the costume shop which was her destination. She sighed gratefully, lowering her arms with the muff in one hand, the richly wrapped parcel in the other. This was the "costume house," this brown, ragged-looking, big square house. Even in the uncertain light, the paler flecks of an old coat of paint showed in jagged patches.

The number would be over the door, no doubt, but there was no need to puzzle over this. Nailed against one of the trees which grew close to the public walk was a sign, its gilt letters shining faintly: *Brit's Costumes.*

"Well, Judy, my girl," the fur-clad figure addressed herself with a rueful sigh, "you're here."

She looked at the walk leading to the entrance, at more ice over uneven cement, and at the dejected steps. Finally the house itself claimed a quick scrutiny. It was far, far from what Judy Garland had expected to find at the end of her friendly mission. There was a porch, its screens torn, furniture stacked haphazardly against all sides. There were windows, some blacked out with a dark brownish paint, the others winking fretfully through listless, ruffled curtains.

"It serves you right," Judy berated herself, walking closer to the sagging steps, "for leaving the word *NO* out of your vocabulary. Berta could have sent this gift just as easily—"

She paused, the picture of Berta Patton coming

to mind: "Big Berta Patton," whose heart was as big as her own generous self, who had turned one real estate venture after another into a remarkably successful business, but who had never outgrown her humblest friends.

Judy smiled swiftly, thinking of Berta. What she had requested seemed a little thing. Judy was passing through this northern city, so would she please deliver this Christmas gift to Mrs. Dora Brit? That was Berta's older sister. She had a costume shop. She was a great-grandmother, and she made wonderful historical dolls in authentic dresses of their period.

The way Berta told it, Dora Brit was every bit as successful in her work as Berta had been. But the sisters had not seen each other in years. Berta could have no idea that this tumbledown old house was her supposedly successful sister's "establishment." It certainly looked far from prosperous, Judy thought.

But did it matter? Judy answered herself swiftly—of course it didn't matter. It had taken more time for Judy to deliver the parcel as a personal messenger for Berta Patton, and time was precious, but a gift delivered "by hand" was certain to arrive safely when so many things were delayed or even lost. Doing a good deed for Berta, who did so much for everybody else, was a pleasure. And perhaps, now that Judy saw how Dora Brit lived—in such a rundown place as this—perhaps the gift would be all the more joyously received.

Judy's gloved finger found the bell and pressed it. There was no ringing sound from within, but a light gleamed suddenly inside, and voices came, mingled and muffled. The door opened, and Judy stepped swiftly aside to let two people out—a middle-aged couple. The man carried a bulky package. He was laughing—a deep, booming sound.

"Don't you worry, I'll put in plenty of pillows. I always wanted to be Santa Claus!" he was saying.

The man and woman clung together, ready to descend the steps. Judy moved closer to the door, which was still open, revealing another woman—a short woman with dull gold hair. Her short nose, blue eyes, and wide mouth told Judy at once that this was Dora Brit, Berta's sister. She was older than Berta certainly, and a woman who counted pennies to Berta's dollars, but she was also clearly a woman who was happy in her work.

Judy thought fleetingly, "I'm glad I came!" She said aloud, speaking eagerly, "Mrs. Brit?"

"I'm Mrs. Brit," the woman acknowledged and nodded, her lips still framing the smile she had sent after the departing couple. One hand stuffed a wadded bill in the pocket of her faded smock, while she beckoned with the other for Judy to enter.

The girl came in, and the door closed after her. They stood in a square room. A stairway led upward, and at the foot was a high, carved cabinet. The doors were open and Judy saw the array of dolls, or rather, the assorted heap of them. A high window cut deeply into another wall, and on the ledge were more dolls, of every size and description. A wide door led into what had been intended for a living-room, but which was now filled with great round racks where costumes of all kinds hung on wire hangers.

Judy's glance had been swift, but the old woman followed it.

"This is a madhouse," she said, lifting a wisp of golden hair and tucking it behind one ear.

Her hair was a little too golden, Judy reflected, but why not? Dora Brit's face had few wrinkles, and those that cut in around her eyes and mouth were the "laughing kind." She looked like a very likable person.

Judy smiled understandingly. "It's a busy time of the year, isn't it? Almost Christmas—"

"Busy!" Dora exploded mildly. "I just rented out my last Santa Claus costume. To Doctor Johnson! He'll be grand!" She seemed to become really aware of Judy, of her fur coat, of the tiny matching fur hat and muff, of the extravagant parcel in her hands. "You wanted something?" she asked, and the smile seemed to wipe itself from her face, leaving a look of deep bewilderment. "Don't tell me you're Judy Garland!"

"I'm afraid I have to tell you that," Judy laughed merrily. "You see—I *am* Judy Garland."

"Heavenly day!" Dora put one hand on the girl's

arm. "I was just going to do you!"

"To *do* me?" It was Judy's turn to be puzzled, and Dora's turn to laugh.

"In a doll," she explained. She gave a wide gesture toward the cabinet, the window ledge. "That's only part of them," she said. "I make 'em to sell, but my son says it's just an excuse I use to make 'em. I don't really *want* to sell them."

"They're just darling!" Judy said enthusiastically. "I wish I could stay to see them all, but it took me rather longer than I thought to get here. I took the wrong bus, and walking's terrible in the slush."

"Isn't it, though?" Dora sympathized. "It's turning colder, and the streets'll be sheets of ice." But it was evident that the woman's tongue prattled words which only lightly hid her greater interest—a wide-eyed wonderment that Judy Garland should be in this humble costume shop. Her blue eyes went again to the girl's face. "You didn't come to rent a costume?" she asked, faintly uneasy.

"Not this time." Judy's quick smile flashed. She lifted the package, bright with its silver ribbon and shining blue stars. "I came to give you this. It's from Berta."

"From—Berta?" Dora's hands waited. "You mean—my sister Berta?"

"That's right. I was coming through here, and she asked me to deliver it in person, to be sure you'd get it in time. And she wanted me to give you her love and tell you everything is just wonderful."

The simple, small words poured from Judy's lips, words you might use in speaking to a hurt child. Because Dora Brit seemed suddenly to shrink within herself, struggling to hide her feelings, and failing dismally. Judy saw the first flash of joy that lighted the blue eyes, but she saw, too, the quivering hands that took the package, heard the sharp intake of the old woman's breath.

To tide over the uncomfortable moment, Judy talked on. "Berta said she wished you could come to visit her, but she supposes it is impossible now. She's been planning to visit you—"

"Planning to visit *me*?" Dora cut in sharply. "Is she coming—*now*?"

"Oh, no. She can't."

What was the matter with the golden-haired woman? Berta had imagined she would be so happy to have direct news, and to receive the gift placed right in her hands. But Dora Brit looked like a different person since the mention of her sister's name. She actually appeared to be *afraid* Berta was coming, and deeply relieved to know that she couldn't come.

Judy felt frustrated, as though she had suffered a letdown. She had gone out of her way to perform a kindly act, in the holiday spirit, only it had turned out quite differently from what she had expected. The room seemed suddenly very stuffy, even oppressive. Judy wanted to get out—to escape into the chill open air.

She made a move toward the door, ready to explain the necessity of her leaving, when the woman put down the gift, tucking it swiftly into the open cabinet and shutting the door.

"Wait," she begged. "I want to talk to you. Just a moment." Her gaze went swiftly up the stairs, came to Judy's face. She motioned to the room filled with costumes. "In here," she said, her hand on Judy's arm to indicate the way.

They passed through the archway, but once they were near the racks, they drew apart, the older woman preceding the girl. At the far end of the room was a low bench.

"Let's sit down here," Dora Brit said, and in a confused state of mind Judy obeyed.

"You'll think I wasn't glad you came," the old woman said in a rush. "But I am. I'm very glad. It was just that I—well, I don't want Berta to know." She looked beseechingly into the girl's wide dark eyes. "She *doesn't* know, does she?"

"Know *what*, Mrs. Brit?"

"That I have a place—," her eyes ran lightly toward the racks, "—like this. A cheap, junky shop."

"Why, it isn't cheap and junky!"

"Oh, yes it is." A low chuckle that was not from enjoyment ran through the words. "It's cheap, all right. I rent my costumes from seventy-five cents to a dollar and a half apiece. But that's the way I started in this business. That's what my customers come here to pay. And they keep on coming, again and again."

"I'm sure they do," Judy put in, somewhat at a loss, but eager to bring comfort. With an effort she stilled the impulse to put her arms around the bent shoulders. "You have—so many costumes."

"Over two thousand. There're five more cupboards in the back rooms, and three racks upstairs." The woman's gaze went in the direction of the stairs. "My grandson lives up there, him and his little girl. Elsie, too, that's his wife. She's a sweet little thing. They like the shop and help me all they can. It's James—"

"James?"

"That's my own boy, my son. He thinks I'm getting on in years. He thinks I should give all this up and come and live with him."

"I think that would be very hard for you to do," Judy said positively, "when you love it so!"

The glad light shone again in the older woman's eyes. "I do love it. James can't see the kick I get out of it." The golden head nodded. "Yes, *kick*. I visit with my customers, some I've had for years. And you'd be surprised the people who keep a 'Brit Box' on hand and stuff in everything they can't find use for. I give 'em Brit Boxes to save for me any castoffs they don't want—and then they tote it all over here to me. I never would have been able to get those sleighbells for the Santa Clauses—," she paused abruptly. One hand closed over Judy's fingers. "I mustn't rattle on. Only—I don't want Berta to know. I've been afraid that James'd write to her, and between the two of them they'd make me quit."

"I don't see why," Judy said staunchly. "This place is nothing you need to be ashamed of. It's—it's nice and cozy." Suddenly it seemed more cozy than ever, perhaps because the older woman had brightened. "And," Judy went on, "I don't think Berta'd ever want you to leave it, not really. Maybe she has made a lot of money, Mrs. Brit, but *Berta* hasn't changed. She's —well, she's about perfect!"

"Is that right? She hasn't changed?" Dora Brit gave a happy sigh, shook her head in glad remembrance. "Berta's so different from me. I mean, being successful. It's been so long since we've seen each other. You know, you get queer notions when you don't see your people for years and years."

Judy rose. "Well, you don't need to get any notions about Berta, Mrs. Brit. I'm sure she's just the same as she always was as far as you're concerned. And I know she'd like your shop!"

Judy had heard the voices in the small room, and Mrs. Brit became aware, too, that customers had arrived. She stood at Judy's side, listening.

"It's all right," she said. "I don't have to go. Elsie's there to take care of them." She led Judy to the nearest cabinet. "I know you're a busy girl, but I want to show you what I have in here. About the only things that're worth much in the shop—my collection of hats and the May Day dresses!"

"Oh—?" Judy said questioningly on a note of pleasure.

Dora was opening the high, walnut cabinet. "I called 'em *May Day* dresses, because they're not anything in particular. Could do for almost anything that was pretty without being historical." The door was open and the seamed, wrinkled hands reached upward to a heap of hats, caps and bonnets, stroking them with gentle affection. "My mother made this one. And this I cut the back out of. And here's one from the Civil War. A friend of mine had it in her family all those years."

Judy made appropriate remarks of interest and approval. The hats were delightful and foolish things, and, as Dora Brit said, some of them were very valuable. It was easy to see that. But Judy's attention had been drawn to the rack below the shelf where the bonnets were kept. Here were the "May Day dresses," frothy things of pink, blue, green and white. However, there was one rich, creamy satin sleeve that seemed to be thrust inward among the pastel shades, as though the dress had been too hastily put away. That sleeve claimed Judy's alert eye. It was not all satin: much of it was finest net, and the two materials were encrusted, at the seams where they met, with tiny seed pearls.

Judy had removed her gloves. She thrust them into her muff and her fingers took a gentle hold of the oddly interesting sleeve to bring it out.

"This is lovely!" she said. "May I see it?"

"Why—yes." Dora Brit spoke hesitantly.

She pushed the hangers aside to free the creamy satin, reached in and brought out the long gown.

"Oh!" Judy's soft cry held delight. "It's—beautiful!" She was not looking at Dora Brit as she held the garment, feasting upon the material, the delicate workmanship. The bodice was softly draped, with a deep insertion of the net, and it carried a rose design of the pearls all the way down to meet the richly draped waist. The skirt fell simply, in folds so soft that only a master costumer could have achieved the elegant grace of it.

"It's—beautiful!" Judy said again, holding the dress lovingly over her two hands. She turned eagerly to the older woman. "This didn't come out of one of your Brit Boxes, did it?"

She stopped when she saw the blank astonishment on the other's face.

"I—I don't know where that dress did come from!" Dora Brit said slowly. "I never saw it before!" One hand went to her hair, pushing it back again. She seemed dazed, as though in a dream. "I—I can't understand it!" she murmured.

"Maybe one of the others put it in here," Judy offered. She felt again a wish to help Dora Brit, to set her tumbled world aright. "I mean, one of your family."

"No." The woman shook her head. "They'd have told me." She stared at the trailing satin. "Nothing like that's ever come into *my* shop!"

It was an awkward moment. Judy stood uncertainly, holding the lovely garment. She was acutely conscious of Dora Brit's bewilderment, and of something even more strange.

The woman was afraid!

Judy made a move to replace the dress in the rack. "Maybe the owner will show up," she offered, and the suggestion sounded weak in her own ears. "A gown like this *must* have an owner," she tried to add lightly. "It's certain to be claimed."

But Dora Brit only became more tense. Her eyes, staring at the creamy satin, seemed to tear away, to look into the other, smaller room, where Elsie was sending away another well-satisfied customer. The outer door opened, and closed.

Elsie called, "Mother–?"

Dora moistened her lips. "I'm in here–with a customer," she said almost naturally. "You run on upstairs, Elsie. I'm almost finished."

The unseen Elsie said a grateful word of agreement and her footsteps sounded, ascending the stairs.

Dora Brit turned swiftly to Judy. "It must have been the girl—last week. I remember, a girl came in with a package—."

"Oh." Judy let herself relax. "You do know who

brought it, then."

"I'm pretty sure I know." But the tension had not lessened for Dora Brit. Rather, it had become intensified. Her lips were pursed, her brows furrowed with the force of her thoughts, seeking back through the days, trying to recall the details of how she had acquired that costume. "She had a package when she came in, and I'm sure she didn't have it when she went out—only the doll she bought."

"She bought a doll?" Judy brightened. "Then you must remember her. Maybe you know her name."

"I do, or I'll have it in a minute. Anyhow, I wrote it down. I have a funny notion, wanting to know who buys my dolls. James says you'd think they were my children out for adoption." The mouth set more firmly. "I don't sell to everybody. I can't help the way I feel about my dolls. But this girl was—nice. She had golden hair, the kind of hair I had when I was a girl. Her name was—Frederica. That's it, Frederica Hammond."

"Do you know her address?" Judy asked.

"No, I don't. But her name is a help." Dora Brit looked again at the satin gown which Judy still held. "I'll bet anything it was she who brought it in," the woman went on. "I remember I found the paper in here a day or so after. It was shoved in under this rack here, right next to the cabinet." A frown cut in again between her eyes! "But why should she bring a thing like that in here? And hide it like that?"

Judy shook her head. "I can't imagine. Unless she wanted to give it to you."

"Give it to me?" the woman repeated almost gruffly. "No, not like that. I like to have my gifts handed to me free and open, so I know whom to thank."

Someone was coming in again. Judy noticed that people came in, not as though entering a private home but as they would enter a place of business. There was no knocking at the door.

"Anybody here?" a woman called out. "Oh, Dora—!"

"Just a minute." Dora Brit excused herself to Judy. "I'll get Elsie to come down and find out what she wants. Please wait."

Judy stood quietly for several minutes while Dora spoke to the customer, saw to it that Elsie took care of her needs. Hastily, then, she returned to Judy's side.

Her voice had been cheerful in the other room, but there was little of cheer about Dora Brit now. She came close to Judy, took one of her hands over the folds of the mysterious dress.

"I can't have James see that," she said in a whisper. "I can't have that gown here! Will you do something for me, Miss Garland? Will you take the dress back to that girl who brought it and left it here?"

Judy's lips parted. "Wh-Why," she hesitated, "I have no idea—"

"I know I'm asking you to do a favor when you don't know me." the woman said urgently. "But I don't know what else to do. I'm at my wit's end!"

"Couldn't we call her up? Find out first if she did leave it here?"

"Oh, she did! It was this Frederica Hammond and no mistake. She looked like the kind of a girl that might bring in something like that. And I know for sure she came in with a package, and all she had when she left was the doll, the little Dutch girl doll. About ten boys came in when she was ready to go, elves they were, and I got so busy I never thought about what she had. But I know it must have been her!"

Judy looked uncertainly at the beautiful satin folds. "I'd like to help you," she said, "but—"

"*Please*, Miss Garland!" Dora Brit's fingers pressed against Judy's fur-clad arms. "I know it's a lot to ask of a stranger, and it seems foolish that I'm asking it. But if this costume's found around here, it might mean the end of this business for me. James is just waiting for some excuse to make me quit—"

"But you haven't *done* anything!" Judy protested. "How could anyone blame you for finding a costume in your shop that somebody just up and left?"

Dora Brit shook her head. "You don't understand, my dear. I'm an old woman. Things are different with me. James means well enough. Sometimes that's all the worse, when your children are grown and they mean well. It—it wouldn't take you long to look up her address. You could call her, or send it to her—

"Please, Miss Garland," Mrs. Brit Begged

anything to get it out of here before any of *them* see it!"

Judy could not ignore the pleading. After all, it was not a difficult thing that Dora Brit was asking her to do. After all, Dora Brit was Berta's *sister*, even if she did act queer. Having the costume out of the way seemed to mean so much to Dora. It would be a simple errand, really. It would not take much of her time.

Or so it seemed to Judy—then.

"Get a piece of paper," Judy said hastily. "Wrap it up and I'll take it!"

The woman seemed to melt with relief and gratitude.

"Oh, bless you!" she said fervently. For an instant, she cocked a listening ear in the direction of the voices. "They're going into the sewing-room," she said softly. "I'll slip out and get the wrapping paper. Wait here."

Again, Judy waited, holding the satin garment affectionately over her two hands. She was conscious of being warm in the room and thought fleetingly that she should take off her coat. Her fingers felt numb, from holding the dress so carefully, and the numbness extended up into her arms. Well, she had been standing here as tense as a coiled spring with this unexplainable lovely garment in her arms.

Judy's thoughts were a dull, beating whirl. She felt caught, helpless, incapable of clear decision. Everything seemed unreal, as in a nightmare—yet this wasn't really a *bad* dream.

"It *is* stuffy in here," she told herself sensibly. "When I get outdoors, I'll feel better."

Presently she heard the crackle of paper, and Dora Brit returned. Her movements were stealthy, but swift. With a few expert motions, she folded the gown, placed the paper over it. From the pocket of her smock, she took out a length of string and tied the package. It was plain, of course—nothing like the gift package Judy had brought into the house, but it reminded Dora of the gracious errand which had brought Judy into her shop.

"Thank you, my dear," she said, as they went back toward the door. "For this favor you are doing for me—and for bringing me Berta's present. I'll write to her. And give her my love, won't you? Tell her—tell her *everything is just fine.*"

In spite of her uneasiness, Judy had to smile.

"I'll tell her," she promised, and without being seen by any of the customers or by the girl, Elsie, Judy went out into the chill evening. On the steps of the ramshackle house she paused for an instant, breathing the fresh air into her lungs. It was a tonic for her depressed mood. She went on down the steps to the sidewalk. She reflected upon the gift she had brought from Berta to Dora—the magnificent lace tablecloth which Berta had sent, and which Dora Brit had not as yet unwrapped. Where would such a costly cloth be used in Dora Brit's house? Did Dora even have a dining-room? Every room in the place must be filled with cabinets of costumes.

Judy considered the package she was bringing away, the satin dress which she had pointed out and which had caused the woman such consternation.

Why had Frederica Hammond left it there? Was that really the girl's name? *Was there really anyone named Frederica Hammond?*

Judy shivered, conscious of the cold winter air. An imp was in the wind, tugging at her brown curls, nipping her ankles. "Goodness," she thought, "this is no place to figure the puzzle out." Nor would it be wisdom to return to her hotel.

The streets were gray-gleaming ice, reflecting the lights that had come on to illuminate the wintry dusk. Ahead, on the corner, was a drugstore.

"I'll go in there and look in the directory," she said half aloud. "I'll call up Frederica Hammond and ask her about it. Maybe I can mail it right from there."

But suppose she did not find Frederica Hammond listed in the directory? What should she do then?

Judy's hands were around the package, warm inside her muff where she had stuffed it, but a different kind of chill from that caused by the wind ran through her being. She felt a sudden dislike for the satin gown, a fervent wish to be rid of it.

"There *has* to be a Frederica Hammond!" she said defiantly against the sting of the wind as she made her way toward the winking lights of the drugstore.

CHAPTER TWO

SWEET AND SMART

The corner on which the drugstore was located was also marked to show it was a bus and streetcar stop. Perhaps a dozen would-be passengers waited at the curb, scanning the street. In the light from the brilliant display windows, the waiting people all appeared to huddle in their heavy clothing.

As Judy drew nearer, she remembered that her face was known to millions. She took a handkerchief from the purse compartment of her muff, managed a convincing cough, and kept the linen over her lips. It was not much of a mask, but it had served its purpose before, and would perhaps suffice now, when she had no wish to be recognized.

She had little difficulty in passing those who waited on the sidewalk, but there were others crammed into the space inside the door, a group of people not staunch enough to brave the sharp wind. Coughing again to excuse the handkerchief she kept well over her face, Judy edged her way into the store.

She passed the candy counter, heard the dismayed voice of a woman bewailing the absence of chewing gum, and came near the soda fountain. Someone brushed against her, jostling her hand from her face.

Quickly, she replaced the handkerchief and made her way along a counter displaying an assortment of bright Christmas cards.

She looked frantically for a telephone booth and at last glimpsed one. With a sigh of relief she hurried toward it.

But, in the tradition of all public telephones, this one was in use. What was more annoying, the telephone directory was inside the booth. Judy felt a pang of disappointment. She wanted to rush in and look up the name of Frederica Hammond. She wanted to call Miss Hammond and find out now, at once, if she was the girl who left the gleaming satin gown at Brit's. If Miss Hammond admitted the gown belonged to her, Judy would see that it was returned with all possible speed.

She did not have time to spare, it was true. But that wasn't all. Judy was obsessed with an inexplicable, driving necessity to be rid of the dress. The paper crackled almost viciously against the fur of her coat. The package seemed to take on a burdensome weight, growing heavier every second.

She came closer to the booth. The woman inside was still talking. Tapping one toe impatiently, Judy looked away, and caught the image of herself in a full-length mirror. The girl she saw reflected there, with the handkerchief over her lips, was herself, and yet it was not the girl she saw in her own mirror at home. The dark eyes that now stared back at her were wide with alarm.

"This won't do!" Judy thought. "I'm getting panicky—and it's just silly!"

Some of the comforting words she had spoken to Dora Brit came back to reproach her. The older woman of the costume shop had done nothing of which she needed to feel ashamed or afraid. She had not stolen the beautiful, old-fashioned gown—it had come to her shop without her knowledge. It had been simply thrust upon Dora, and upon Judy, too. A strange, gloriously beautiful dress had got into a shop by mistake, and she, Judy Garland, had been asked by a kindly old lady—a grandmotherly lady—to take it back to the rightful owner. What could be wrong in that? Why should she feel furtive and, yes, guilty—like some thief in the night?

The dark eyes in the mirror became softer. "Pretty soon I'll have the old thing off my hands," Judy thought, "and that will be—that."

The woman came out of the booth at last, and Judy quickly slipped inside. Placing her muff and the package on the small shelf, the girl leafed through the directory.

The name was there: *Frederica Hammond, 1864 Marshall Ave.*

What a relief it was to know she wasn't dreaming, after all! Judy delved into one of the side pockets of her coat, an easily reached place for small change. The nickel fell with a gay clink into its slot, and Judy dialed the number with a steady finger. She had completely regained her usual self-composure.

Almost immediately, a voice answered, "Hello?"

"Is Miss Frederica Hammond in?" Judy asked.

The voice repeated, "Hello?"

"Please may I speak to Frederica Hammond? Is this Miss Hammond?"

Judy's pulse fluttered. She had an immediate intuition that it was not the girl she sought who said again and again, with irritating repetition, the metallic sounding word: "Hello? Hello!"

"I want to speak to Frederica Hammond!" But Judy knew she was wasting time. The telephone must be out of order.

"I can't hear you!" the voice came, stringier, fainter. "Who is this speaking? Hello?"

Judy hung up the receiver dejectedly and stood for a moment staring in dismay at the black curve of the mouthpiece.

Now what?

But she knew. She must take the dress to Miss Hammond's address herself in her role of messenger girl. And she must get a cab. For if she stopped to inquire how to get to Marshall Avenue she would attract unwanted attention. No cab had been available when she wanted to go to Brit's. The bus had been quicker than waiting. But this was different, somehow—and time was passing.

Judy looked in the classified section, found the

list under Taxis, and luck favored her. A cab stand was close by. Judy put in the call, gave the name of the drugstore, said she would be waiting on the corner across the street. A man's deep voice assured her that a cab would be on the spot in less than fifteen minutes.

"Well," Judy thought as she let the receiver fall into place, "that's something." She gathered up her muff and the annoying package. "We're going places!" she told the crackling paper. Suddenly, she had an impulse to laugh. Why not? Why not laugh? It was far better to smile than to go on looking like a scared rabbit. She had learned Frederica Hammond's address, and the gown would soon be back where it had come from.

Feeling much more lighthearted than when she had come into the store, Judy made her way out again, attracting as little notice as possible. She crossed the street, arriving at a corner where a food market teemed with a last-minute rush, but where no one was waiting for transportation. Alone in the sea of hurrying shoppers, Judy stood, watching for the taxi.

It was a long fifteen minutes, but when the cab finally came Judy felt it was worth the wait. She sank back into the warmth of the back seat, and gave the woman at the wheel the Marshall Avenue number.

"Is it far?" Judy then asked.

"Not very. About three miles."

Judy sighed and let herself be blissfully comfortable while the car skirted around and streaked through the traffic. They made innumerable turns, leaving the shopping district behind, coming to a wide street with a narrow strip of parkway down the center. The houses on either side were set high on steep banks. Judy did not need to watch for numbers, nor did she try. She heard the driver suddenly say, "Here we are," and they stopped at the curb from which steps went up to a white frame house—a cheerful, neat-looking house.

Judy's spirits rose. The house, at least, looked friendly and harmless. She paid the fare, hurried out and up the steps. The wind seemed to have lessened its biting chill and flakes of snow were beginning to fall. But it was still very cold.

The first time Judy rang the bell, there was no answer. While the girl waited after the second attempt, she became conscious again of the cold. She moved her weight hastily from one foot to the other, trying to keep warm, and was grateful when a light flashed through the glass in the door.

A tall woman opened it, a woman who might be forty or sixty years of age, plain of feature but with vivid dark eyes and a mass of dark hair. She wore a baker's white apron over a wine-colored woolen dress. The moment she said, "Yes?" Judy knew it was the voice she had heard over the telephone.

"I came to see Frederica Hammond," Judy explained, smiling. "Is she here?"

"No, but won't you come in? It's so cold."

Judy went gratefully inside. "When do you expect Miss Hammond?" she asked.

"I'm sorry, but I don't know."

"She won't be here this evening?" Judy asked, and her voice seemed to ring hollowly in the big room where she found herself.

The tall woman shook her head. She was about to speak when, from another room, a voice called, "Who is it, sister?"

"Someone asking for Miss Hammond," the tall woman replied, as a rosy-cheeked woman in a red-checked housedress came into view.

"That's too bad." The head with its white ringlets shook with real regret "Miss Hammond left—" she began, and her mouth opened with amazement. "Why, it's Judy Garland the movie star, Grace!" She came nearer, head on one side, peering at the girl. "That's who she is!"

Judy had no intention of prolonging any question of her identity. "I am Judy Garland, yes," she confessed. "And I'd like so much to see Frederica. Do you know where I could reach her?"

The white-haired lady said nothing, but continued to regard the girl with unfeigned delight—almost with reverence. It was the tall woman who spoke: "Come and sit down, Miss Garland." She led the way across the long living-room to the sedate fire burning in a narrow fireplace. "You'll have to excuse me for not recognizing you," she apologized, "but I don't go to the movies very much."

"But I do!" the glowing white-haired woman said. "Oh, I'm sorry Frederica isn't here. Are you a friend of hers? She never told us!"

The tall woman saved Judy from answering. "We're the Doyles," she explained "This is my sister, Marion, and I'm Grace." It was said somewhat pointedly, as though tall, dark Grace were mildly reprimanding her sister for imprudent questioning.

Judy said, "How do you do?" Her eyes went over the room, plain but comfortable, though she scarcely saw what was in it, her thoughts being centered upon the girl she sought. "Can you tell me how I could reach Frederica?" she asked of them both. "I have a—a gift for her." She indicated the package. "And I haven't so very much time."

Both the women had seated themselves, Marion on the couch at the girl's side, Grace on a near-by upholstered rocker.

Grace said, "She's gone out to her aunt's house—Mrs. Mattis. Do you know her?"

Judy shook her head. "No, I don't," she said.

"She's been very ill," Marion put in. "Last week they called up and asked if Frederica would come. And Frederica went, of course, though I don't know why she should! *They* never seemed to care much what happened to *her*!"

"Marion!" Grace remonstrated, but the white-haired woman only shrugged.

"It's true!" Marion said, as though waters, held back too long, burst forth. "You know Frederica," she appealed to Judy. "What a sweet girl she is. And *smart*. And everything she's got, she got by her own efforts. *They* never cared. Not until Mrs. Mattis became really sick. Then Frederica was good enough, all right. She had to go out there and play nurse—when she needed this vacation so much!"

Once more Judy found herself in the midst of confusion. The women were taking it for granted that because she was bringing a "gift" to Frederica, she must know all about the girl. Judy was at a loss for words. She could not retract the "gift" that had innocently slipped from her mouth. But what else could she say? That she had a ravishingly lovely satin gown which Frederica Hammond had stealthily hidden among the cheap costumes at Brit's Costume Shop, and that she, Judy Garland who had no connection with Brit's, was returning it?

Judy said, truthfully enough, "I didn't know about Frederica's aunt. I—I didn't know she was taking a vacation."

"She isn't," Marion Doyle said hotly, and her pink cheeks grew pinker. Judy realized that though her hair was snowy white she was the younger of the sisters. "Frederica's not having any vacation at the Mattis house," Marion went on emphatically. "You can't tell me she is!"

"How can you say that?" Grace asked her. (Judy guessed that the two had argued this point before.) "Maybe they're really waking up, Marion."

"Not *them*!" Marion said stubbornly. "They could have helped her before this!" She appealed to Judy. "You know Frederica hasn't any people, not immediate relatives, I mean. She's been an orphan since she was about twelve. That aunt of hers is rich. She could have done so much for the girl." Her voice changed abruptly. "Not that Frederica's been one to complain. In all the four years she's been here, she never once said a word against them!"

"And she never said much either way," Grace put in. "Most of this is your imagination, Marion." Grace now claimed Judy's attention. "Frederica's had the best luck, Miss Garland. You'll be glad to know that she's going to do the layout for Maley's after the first of the year. My, how she can draw those fashion ads!"

Judy had felt helplessly like a straw caught upon a turbulent sea, being dashed willy-nilly this way and that. But when she heard that Frederica drew "fashion ads," she recognized a possible connection with the satin gown. Whatever Frederica's history had been, the only way that she, Judy, fitted into the pattern, was in the returning of the garment. She turned suddenly to Marion at her side.

"Have you seen the little Dutch girl doll that Frederica bought?" she asked eagerly.

And Marion's reply came with refreshing haste.

"Oh, yes! You knew about that! It's the dearest thing! She has it up there in her boudoir." The white head indicated the stairs which rose at the far end of the room. "When Frederica came, she just rented one room from us," she went on. "But after awhile, she had to have more space. For her drawings, you know. And she liked to cook. So we fixed the pink and the blue rooms into a kitchenette. Frederica's got it so nice now. She even has her own telephone up there!" Marion looked at Grace. "I hope they can fix it before she gets back."

Her own telephone! Judy knew that, though. She had found the girl's name readily in the directory. And she had now confirmed the fact that Frederica Hammond had actually purchased the little Dutch girl doll. So, beyond a doubt, it was she who had left the satin gown at Brit's Costume Shop.

Judy heard Grace murmur some word of mild reproach to Marion, but the girl was not listening. The polite smile on her lips shielded her thoughts, which were racing wildly.

Should she leave the package here with the two women? Ask them to keep it for Frederica until the girl should return from her aunt's?

Some small inner voice whispered faintly, urgently, "No. No, don't tell them!"

The only reason Judy had for not telling them was that the lovely garment had come to Brit's in a hasty, furtive way. Mrs. Dora Brit had not received it with gratitude, but with apprehension, and fear. What was the secret the dazzling dress had to reveal? There was something terribly disturbing about the whole business.

A small sigh escaped Judy's lips. She drew one hand across her forehead, seeking to clear the tumble of her pounding thoughts. Marion misinterpreted the gesture.

"You're tired—and I'll bet you're hungry!" she said, coming closer to the girl. "Won't you have supper with us? We were just going to have a bite in the kitchen. Grace has to go back to the office again tonight." Marion's white head bobbed in the direction of her older sister.

"Grace is the man-of-the-house," she explained. "She has a job while I take care of the place."

The dark woman received this tribute with a mild grunt, as though she had often heard Marion calling her the wage-earner—as though, perhaps, she somewhat regretted the necessity, but endured it as her lot in life.

Judy looked at the two of them, fully and directly, really seeing them for the first time. The absent Frederica, whom they believed to be a friend of hers, had so clouded her worried mind, that she had not realized how really kind these women were. And, though there might be some nagging mystery clouding the head of the girl Judy had not yet seen, there was nothing fantastic or dream-worldish about this

"You're Tired," Marion Said, Seeing Judy's Gesture

pair. Nor was there anything alarming about their asking her to stay to supper. For, though Grace had not spoken, the invitation was shining from her eyes.

Judy smiled at them. "I *am* hungry," she said. "And I think I smell biscuits—don't I?"

Marion came to her feet. "Oh, my biscuits! I completely forgot! But I was so pleased to see you, Miss Garland! So glad to know you're a friend of Frederica's! She has so many wonderful friends—!"

Grace said in a patient voice, "Better get out to the kitchen, Marion. I'll show Miss Garland to Frederica's rooms. Then I'll be down to help you."

Marion went out in a flurry of excited delight. Grace looked at Judy, and a warm current of understanding flowed between them.

"Marion hasn't had this much fun since Frederica brought home her artist," Grace said, her hand on the girl's arm, propelling her to the stairs. "Go right on up," she said. "Frederica's rooms are at the left of the hallway. Marion was cleaning in there today, and the door's still unlocked. You can tidy up and get your breath. Come on down when you're ready."

"Oh, thank you," Judy said gratefully. "It'll take me only a few minutes."

As she mounted the stairs, the fragrance of the biscuits floated up, warmly inviting. It was going to be fun to stay to supper with the Doyles, Judy thought. They were as friendly a pair as she could remember ever having met.

And Frederica must be nice, too. "Sweet" and "smart," Marion had said. Besides, you could see how both the women loved her.

But Marion was worried about Frederica, for some reason. Although she could not prove it, Judy was certain of it.

Here was the door. Judy opened it and a little cry of delight came softly to her lips. The downstairs portion of the Doyle home had made no deep impression upon her. There were tables and chairs and pictures. But Frederica Hammond's room was quite another thing.

The paper on the walls was gray with a blue-and-white stripe. Drapes at the windows were decorated with delicate flower sprays—palest green, deep pink, and rose. The carpet was a deep-piled delicate green. And there were many shelves; a quaint, low desk; a table where Frederica must do her art work; two white chairs. And everywhere were funny little figures, vases, statues, a fascinating variety of small treasures. The room might almost be called an artist's toy shop, but still it was not cluttered-looking. It was simply delightful.

Judy's eyes roved about until they rested on something that might have seemed out of place, but could never be, because a faded and tattered *teddy bear* was a treasure of dear remembrance, to be esteemed in any setting. Judy felt drawn to the bear. She went closer to where it was propped against the side of a low cabinet.

"Poor bear," she said softly. "You look chewed to pieces."

Above the sad brown of its ears an enlarged snapshot hung on the wall. It was of a black Scottie.

"So," Judy met the quizzical, suspicious eye. "YOU did the chewing!" In that instant, Judy Garland felt her heart going out to a girl she had never known, a girl who became an orphan when little more than a child. A girl who had bravely faced the disinterest of wealthy kinsfolk and had built for herself a delightful hodge-podge of a room that was her very own. And more—she had made a worthwhile career for herself.

But the Doyles had said "rooms." Judy slipped off her coat, let it fall onto one of the white chairs, placed the package near it, and undertook a tour of exploration. There was a bedroom, almost all in white, with touches of pink and silver in the wallpaper, palest blue in the frothy curtains. There was a bathroom in green and blue, with merry-eyed sea horses and fat, bubble-blowing fish swimming all over the four walls. And a kitchen! Literally, there was just enough room for Judy to turn around in it. Judy peeked into the red-and-white cupboards, opened the ice-box, lifted the lid from the electric stove. What a place in which to play house!

But moments were flashing by. Guiltily, Judy hurried to suds her face and hands, to run a comb through her thick curls, to apply fresh lip rouge. And she felt immeasurably refreshed as she came down the stairs.

Both the sisters were waiting for her. Marion gave a little cry of pleasure at the sight of the girl. Judy was wearing a wool dress of dull green, of Chinese cut. Flat, gold buttons went from the high neck, curving down the full length of the frock. It was a comfortable dress—and warm.

Marion said, "You looked wonderful in your fur coat, Miss Garland. But that shade of green—!" She paused for lack of words, and Grace said, practically, "And those golden biscuits! Come, Miss Garland, and find out what an excellent cook Marion is."

They passed through a long, narrow room—the dining-room—into the cheerful cream-and-white kitchen. Judy glanced at the table, covered with a strawberry-spattered cloth. There were the biscuits, indeed! And scrambled eggs! And several kinds of jam!

"There are more in the oven," Marion said, and went to the white stove.

Judy laughed. "*More?* Why this is enough for anybody!"

And it was, too. Judy ate heartily. Marion talked mostly of her favorite recipes and of the canning she had done. And how glad she was that she had learned to be a good gardener.

Only when they had finished, did Judy realize how quiet Grace had been throughout the meal. Glancing at the dark woman suddenly, Judy caught a glimpse of the downcast eyes, the frown that lined the high, rugged forehead. Grace, at that moment, looked up, and there passed between the two of them a kind of worried premonition. It was as though Grace had said, "Let Marion enjoy her simple things. You and I know what really lies ahead of us."

Judy shook off her morbid imaginings and came abruptly to the present and her unfinished task. She told the Doyles again how delicious the supper had been, and then begged them to excuse her hasty departure.

Marion asked, "Are you going back to your hotel, Miss Garland?"

Before Judy answered, she asked herself silently, "Am I? Or should I try first to reach Frederica at the home of her aunt?"

Grace seemed to read her mind. "It's too bad you couldn't have seen Frederica," she said, rising. "But then, we haven't been able to see her either."

"Her aunt is sick, you know," Marion put in. "I—I got lonesome to talk to her—to Frederica, I mean—and I called up her aunt's house. The maid, or somebody who answered the phone, said Frederica was with Mrs. Mattis and please not to call again. She said she'd have Frederica call us back. But she hasn't called back—not once."

Grace shrugged. "Perhaps she hasn't had a chance. Anyway, what does it matter, Marion? We have no right interfering with the girl's business." She turned to Judy. "I'd like to give you a lift to your hotel," she said, "if you'll let me."

"Why—," Judy began, intending to say it wasn't at all necessary—when she caught the silent message in the dark woman's eyes: "I have something to tell you. Accept my offer. This is important."

So Judy said, "Why, thank you. That's very kind of you."

Grace nodded, almost with approval. Then she shook her shoulders lightly. "It's not much of a car. But it still goes." She put one hand on the girl's arm. "You run up and get your things and I'll bring the car out in front."

"I'll hurry," Judy promised, and went back upstairs. Her coat was where she had left it, and the package. Hastily she slipped her arms into the soft folds—and became aware that Marion had come into the room.

"I'll turn out the lights now," Marion said. "It's pretty up here, isn't it?"

Judy agreed warmly that it was a pretty room. And she gave a thought to the lights, as she glanced around the sitting-room. There were several small lamps, and one tall one. All were aglow—just as they had been when she had first come in.

"I light 'em every evening for a while," Marion explained in a muffled voice. "It seems to make me feel as though she's coming back every night. I wish she would. She's—almost like our own." As though to forestall her tears, the woman laughed shakily. "Grace and I are a couple of old maids, I guess."

Judy adjusted the band that held the little fur hat firmly on her head. Her fingers fumbled a little, and she found it difficult to meet the woman's eyes. She said, after a small pause, "But Frederica's only visiting her relatives, you know. It's—just a little vacation."

"Yes," Marion admitted, as though hearing words which she wanted to believe. "Yes. It's just a little vacation." She patted Judy's arm. "I hear Grace out in front. You'd better run."

Judy heard the car, too, chugging valiantly. She grabbed up her muff and the crackling paper package. Marion eyed it questioningly, but held her tongue, for which Judy was somehow grateful. It would have been the natural thing for her to leave the gift she had brought for one whom Marion believed to be a good friend. It was hardly surprising for Marion to wonder why Judy was carrying it away again.

The girl took refuge in flight. "Thank you so much," she said, "for everything. If I'm in the city longer than I had planned, I'll try to come out again." There, that might ease the awkward situation—the promise to come again.

"Oh, I wish you would!" Marion urged earnestly. "I hope you see Frederica. She can tell you all about her new job—and everything."

Judy was leaving the room, facing the door that led into the hall, when she saw the door of a half-open cabinet. A doll was sitting sedately inside, a doll in a

Dutch costume, with wooden shoes.

The little Dutch girl doll that Frederica had bought at Brit's!

Somehow, the sight of the doll seemed to bring to life the half-realized fears that had tormented Judy. For she recalled that Frederica might have purchased the doll to cover her stealthy concealing of the satin gown among the other costumes in the Brit shop.

That was what it all came back to—the lovely, radiant satin gown which had sent her on her wanderings this cold winter night. The gown that was folded in the paper which she clasped now.

Judy almost ran down the steps. "Good-bye," she called. "And—thanks again, for everything!"

Marion did not come downstairs. Judy heard her say something which sounded like, "God bless you, my dear," in a choked voice. The white-haired woman was setting about her heart-aching task of putting out the lights in the lonesome, empty room, or perhaps she was openly crying and did not want Judy to see her sentimental tears.

The girl came to the door, opened it. Snowflakes swam in the air around her, endlessly falling. Through their moving white curtain, Judy saw the small car standing at the curb.

She went down the steps, and Grace opened the door.

"Are you sure this isn't too much trouble?" Judy asked.

"Not at all. I was going out anyway. I have work to do." Grace was looking upward at the house, and Judy's eyes followed. The windows of Frederica's rooms went suddenly black. Marion had turned out all the lights.

Did Judy imagine it, or was that a sigh she heard from the dark woman at the wheel of the car? She murmured something under her breath—Judy heard her do that—but the words were muffled, drowned in the rising sound of the motor.

"Where are you staying?" Grace asked loudly. "The Glasson?"

Judy said, "Yes. And I certainly appreciate the ride." She thought, "I seem to have said so often—I'm glad to get a ride. But Grace wanted me to come. She has something to tell me. Something about Frederica. I wish she'd hurry up and say it!"

They were going back over the wide street with its bisecting parkway, going slowly through the blur of the falling snow. Abruptly, Grace broke the silence. "Miss Garland, how much time have you?"

"How much time?" Judy had not expected just this question.

"I mean here. In the city."

"Oh. I am leaving tomorrow."

Grace turned to look at her. "You know," she said slowly, "I'm worried about Frederica. I don't want Marion to know it. But I am."

Here it was. *Frederica.*

"Why?" Judy tried to inquire with the right shade of interest.

"For a number of reasons. The girl's not strong, and she's been working too hard. And now, out there at the Mattis place." Grace turned on the windshield wiper. "I wish she could see you."

"I—I'd like to see her, too," Judy said, and added in her thoughts, "I'd like to get this dress back to her and be finished with all this mystery!"

"I didn't know you and Frederica were friends," Grace went on. "But Frederica has so many wonderful friends. You probably met her before she came to live with us."

Judy could think of no quick answer that would be the truth, so she waited for the woman to continue. Grace went on presently, "I am going to ask you a favor, Miss Garland. Take your gift out to her, to the Mattis place."

"Wh–Why," Judy began to object.

But the woman went on swiftly, "It would mean so much to Frederica. Seeing you," she hesitated briefly, "and another thing, you could give her a message. Tell her that we miss her very much. Would you do that? I think that would bring her home. Anyhow, it would remind her to phone us. It's evident they don't want us to phone her there."

So that was what Grace wanted. Well, after all, it was not an unreasonable request. Believing Judy to be the girl's friend, Grace was right in believing that Judy would want to see her, to deliver into Frederica's own hands the gift Judy had brought.

Judy thought, "I might as well go through with it!" It wasn't as if only one person were involved—there were the Doyle sisters, Frederica herself, and also Mrs. Brit to consider. Judy had as much as pledged her word to Dora Brit that the satin gown should be safely returned to Frederica Hammond.

"Where do the Mattises live?" Judy asked.

Grace said, "You mean *Mrs.* Mattis. From all that I know, she's alone—or was. She lives out south of town, near Lake Oleen." She looked eagerly at the girl. "You're going, then?"

"Yes. It's about seven o'clock now, isn't it?"

"Now?" Grace seemed startled. "My dear, I haven't the time to take you all the way out there!"

"Oh, I didn't mean for you to take me. If you can just get me a cab. Or is it too far? Couldn't I get there tonight?"

"It's a good half-hour's ride, I'd say. But the bus goes right by the door. If only we'd had this talk sooner, I could have driven you out myself!"

"I wouldn't have you bothering!" Judy said firmly. "If you could drop me somewhere near where the bus stops, that'd help. I don't know my way around, you know."

"I'll take you right to the bus stop," Grace promised and her voice was warm, eager. "It'll mean so much to Frederica—and to us." She made a turn to the right.

"I don't know how to thank you."

"You don't need to," Judy said, smiling. "I'll be glad to—to see Frederica."

She would also be glad to give Frederica the satin gown, Judy thought, and the smile on her lips became fixed and frozen, without meaning. "I—I hope they won't mind. I mean, because Mrs. Mattis is ill," Judy said hesitantly.

"Mind?" Grace responded sharply. "How could anyone *mind* having you just drop in for a moment to bring Frederica a present?" The woman sighed deeply. "Oh, I know Frederica will be overjoyed to see you. And you'll be sure to tell her how we miss her, won't you?"

Judy promised to deliver the message. Seven o'clock, she thought. The ride out would take half an hour. By nine, surely, she would be back again, with all her "errands" accomplished. Ruefully, she reflected there had been two such errands heaped upon her in quick succession. First, Berta's lace cloth to be delivered to Dora Brit. Then Dora Brit's unwelcome gown to be delivered to Frederica Hammond. Only it wasn't Dora Brit's. It was Frederica's. Or Frederica had left it at Dora Brit's. Well, soon it would be back where it belonged, and Judy could consider her "girl scouting" over for the time being.

Suddenly, Judy felt a vague tremor of apprehension. It was so simple, and yet the thought had not come to her until this instant.

Would Frederica welcome the return of the glittering gown?

Swiftly, Judy found the answer. No. *No,* the girl could not be grateful for its return. She had wanted to be rid of it, to hide it. That was why she had left it so secretly in the costume shop. Perhaps it was not hers!

But Frederica, from what Judy had learned, from what she had come to believe, was a girl to be admired, someone who surely could be trusted.

Grace was saying something, that they were almost to the bus stop. Judy saw the glowing light on her face, felt the unselfish joy that warmed the dark woman's heart.

"No matter what," Judy thought, "I'll go through with it. I can't help it—even if this mysterious costume *is* jinxed!"

CHAPTER THREE

FORBIDDING RECEPTION

Grace Doyle had taken pains to give Judy full and careful instructions. She was to tell the bus driver that she wished to go to Saint Francis Park, to be let off at 67th Street, at the Mattis place. "He'll know," Grace said positively. "It's a landmark on Lake Oleen. Marion and I have driven past there. It's easy to find. You can't miss it."

Judy had listened attentively, had heard Grace's repetition of her heartfelt gratitude, felt the woman's warm handclasp in farewell.

At last she was on the bus, going to the Mattis house. Grace Doyle, her sister Marion, the friendliness and certainty of a past hour had been replaced in Judy's active mind by a sense of loss.

"What am I really doing here anyway?" Judy asked the self she saw blurred in the misty glass pane of the bus window. "I should be at the hotel, getting a good night's sleep." But here she was, being pushed involuntarily into affairs beyond her knowledge, beyond her choice.

"*No,*" Judy told the face that floated in the glass beside her. "*No!* Will I ever learn to say *no* at the right time?"

But how could she say no, her shadowy eyes asked reproachfully. Not to Berta Patton, and not tc Dora Brit. And the Doyle sisters? She certainly could not say no to them!

It all came back to the package, looking more crumpled now, on the seat beside her. Perhaps, Judy smiled without mirth, *perhaps* Frederica Hammond might wish she *had* refused to deliver this parcel!

Her thoughts drifted, but always came back to center on the puzzle that was Frederica Hammond.

The Doyles loved her, that was evident. They said she was not strong. She had been imposed upon. Her rich relatives had paid no attention to her until Mrs. Mattis was taken sick. Then Frederica was called upon to act as nurse. She had been at the Mattis house since last week. The Doyles' attempt to reach her by telephone had been futile. So—Frederica might be very busy playing nurse. So—she might have forgotten her humbler friends.

But this idea Judy dismissed at once. It was a false note. The Frederica that Marion and Grace knew was a loving and lovable girl, of that she felt confident.

"She *must* be," Judy added in her thoughts. "The chewed teddy bear and the picture of the Scottie. The way she's decorated her rooms—no mean or hateful person would do that."

Judy put one hand to her head, brushing back a thick, brown curl.

What was the good of thinking? Soon she would

be there, seeing Frederica, finding out for herself what the girl was like. More important still, she would at last be free from a responsibility—the paper-wrapped dress—which had become a chore. At last she could return to her comfortable hotel room, to a thick, creamy chenille robe, to small, furry slippers—and *relax!*

Sighing with pleasure at the prospect, she let her eyes drift over the interior of the bus. There were about eight passengers, all sitting near the windows, all gazing out at the lights going by. There was something tired and aimless in the way they watched, something resigned. Judy peered again out the window. The snow was coming down thicker, faster. The other passengers, more weather-wise than she, might sense a coming blizzard.

"Let it come," Judy thought. "I'll be snug in my bed. We must be almost there by now. I'll take the very next bus back."

But Grace Doyle must have miscalculated, or had driven in this direction in fairer weather, for it was a good hour later before Judy heard the driver say, "Here's your stop, Miss."

All the other passengers had left the bus. Judy had watched them go. One by one, they burst out into the night. It almost seemed as though they were eager to brave the cold.

As she waited for the door to open, Judy said, "This must be the end of the line."

"Almost," the bus driver agreed with a grin, and pointed. "See those lights? That's the Mattis—," his mouth dropped open. "Say—!" he began.

But Judy knew what was coming. The old familiar question: *Aren't you Judy Garland?*

She hurried to cut off his flow of words. She heard him say, "I thought when you got on," but heard no more. "Thank you," she said. "I'm sure I'll find it. It's a big place, isn't it?"

The door was open, and the snowy blast entered the warmth, settled in moist dewdrops on the fur coat. The driver said something, but Judy did not hear. She did not hear him try to tell her there would be no returning bus that night unless she were back here again in less than ten minutes!

Her hands in her muff, cradling the package, Judy walked away from the snow-clad highway, over to a kind of sanctuary among a cluster of spruce trees. She looked upward toward the house that loomed before her, and despite the wind and the snow, a smile twisted the girl's mouth.

The Mattis house was, certainly, not hard to find. It stood aloof and alone in what must be grounds the area of a good-sized block. There was a long, curving drive that led upward, around the side of the house, back to another building—an immense garage, with no light showing.

However, lights gleamed in the house, in a tone of deep orange which seemed to reflect against walls

Judy Walked up the Snow-Covered Driveway

of polished mahogany. But the spruce trees interfered with a complete view. Spruce and fir, that grew in clusters, and closer to the great, three-story building appeared to brush against its thick, ancient walls. That it was an old, old house, Judy felt sure, and something more. It was a *lonely* house.

In the small space of time that she stood there, Judy saw more lights come to life on the second floor. Heavily lined drapes, however, clung to the high windows. Only slender wisps of brightness were able to seep through.

Judy felt the tug of the wind, the lash of the driving snow, and reminded herself of the need to move, and to move quickly. But in which direction? There must be three entrances, the front, one at the side, following the curving driveway, and one at the back. Most of the light seemed centered at the side of the house.

Thinking that perhaps she could enter more swiftly there, that perhaps she might find Frederica all the sooner at the side entrance, Judy traced her steps toward the driveway. Her low-heeled shoes were not proof against the four inches of snow that covered the ground. The going was slow and painful. Once she slipped. The package fell, embedded in the snow near the clean, dark circle that outlined a powerful spruce.

"Oh, dear!" Judy ruefully got to her feet, moved over to retrieve the fateful gown. She brushed the paper clear of the clinging flakes and, for a moment, looked about her again. She was nearer the house now, though she could not see it as well, because of the thick trees. But she did make out the massive urns that stood at either side of the front entrance. They might be of cement, and undoubtedly, in the summer, held flowers of some sort, for dried and twisting vines fell over their brims, quivering under the burden of the snow.

The urns were not identical. One was thicker than the other. Or so it seemed until, with a suddenness that completely unnerved the girl, the figure of a man disengaged itself from the urn which was nearest. In the uncertain light, and through the falling flakes, Judy could not tell whether he was young or old, or tall or short. The figure was bending, crouched, ready to leap at her.

Judy had a lightning premonition. The man meant to prevent her entering the house! But he waited, for he did not know that she had seen him. He could not know, for he remained quiet, waiting for her to come nearer, expecting her to cut across to the front entrance.

Fear gave wings to the girl's feet. Blindly she ran along the driveway. She heard a muffled sound, a muted cry of bafflement and rage. Footsteps sounded, coming in pursuit.

Judy ran on, not stopping at the side entrance, for she found it dark. Around at the back of the house, a light gleamed out upon the snow. Centering her hopes upon that light, while her lungs seemed crushed with the weight of the cold air, Judy redoubled her speed until at last she came to the door at the back of the house. It was a storm door, partly open. The girl jerked it wide, found the knob of the inner door, turned it, and leaped inside.

Not till then did she pause, leaning against the closed door, trying to still her wildly beating heart.

Caution advised that she listen, to learn whether her pursuer were still following. Even if he were, her presence had become known in the house. A light flamed in front of her as a door, near at hand, opened. Judy saw, framed before her, the bent shoulders of an elderly woman, a woman who said, "Martin, is that you?" in a husky voice, slow and almost expressionless.

Judy replied shakily, "No. No, it's not Martin." She saw that she stood in an entryway. An immense icebox was at her right, so large that it might have been in some hotel. A cabinet of shelves was at the left, with glass jars, papers, neatly arranged.

"Who *are* you?" said the woman. "What do you want?"

Judy lifted her shoulders away from the door. She stood straight, took a step toward the woman.

"I came to see Frederica Hammond," she said.

There was an instant's pause. The woman seemed not to move an inch. She said, "Miss Hammond—?"

"Yes." Judy edged closer. "Will you please tell her

I'm here?"

Still the woman did not move. "Tell her *who's* here?" she asked.

Judy hesitated. "A friend," she answered, "a friend of the Doyles'. Miss Hammond will understand what I mean."

"Oh," the woman said flatly. "The Doyles."

Judy had regained her composure. Her fear had given place to a rising anger against the net of circumstances which wove itself perversely to thwart her at every turn. "Will you please tell her?" she said, moving to the woman's side. Grudgingly, it seemed, the woman edged herself backward, so that Judy actually entered the kitchen.

The girl sensed that it was a room with high walls, lined part way with white tile. The big sink spread before her, low and wide, all of tile. Near it was a stove which could be used for gas or wood and at the side of it, a row of bright red pots of graduated sizes. At the opposite side of the sink, a short flight of steps led upward.

The woman and Judy were in the kitchen now, standing side by side. Judy saw that the other's hair was thin and wispy and gray, caught up in a knot at her neck. Her features, somehow, matched her voice, flat and uninteresting, revealing very little of her character. But she was old, and bent with years of hard work. A gray cotton uniform hung over her knees, which seemed to bend forward. One-strap, low-heeled button shoes were on broad feet that toed in.

Judy took in all this as she waited for the other woman to speak. But the woman was also taking stock of the girl. Her eyes had been partly closed, eyes that might be a light green or blue—*suspicious* eyes.

She asked, at last, "Does Mr. Frazer know you're here?"

"Mr. Frazer?"

"Yes. Did he say you could come?"

Who, Judy wondered, was Mr. Frazer? The Doyles had not mentioned that name. They had said that Frederica's aunt—Mrs. Mattis—lived alone.

The woman's mouth drew in at the corners. Her arms came up, crossing over her flat chest. "Mr. Frazer said no one was to come in. Not now. So maybe you better go."

"But I can't go!" Judy protested. "I have come to see Frederica. It will only take a moment—."

""What do you want to see her about?" the woman asked.

"It's—it's a personal matter." Judy's dark eyes flashed. "I have to hurry back right away. I won't intrude, I assure you."

She was looking directly into the woman's eyes now and she saw that they were green. The lids were seamed with a mass of tiny wrinkles. But, strangely, while she barred the way, the woman seemed not unkind. Judy sensed that she was not disapproving, really, but that she was repeating orders which she regretted having to enforce.

Judy took advantage of the moment.

"*Please,*" she said, "won't you tell Frederica that I'm here? I've had quite a lot of trouble finding her." Judy glanced backward, toward the entryway. A shaky little laugh escaped her lips. "Someone was out there. Following me. It's a good thing I can run fast!"

The woman's eyes went to the back door. A sigh of resignation came from her lips. "The spirit of the lake," she said, so softly that Judy wondered if she imagined it. But the woman repeated, "The spirit of the lake," and Judy stared at her, startled.

"*He* believes it, and no one else will," the woman went on bleakly. "I wouldn't believe it. All the years I lived by the lake, I never saw the spirit." She seemed to become aware of the girl beside her. "But *you* saw it," she said.

Judy drew a deep breath. "No, I didn't see any spirit," she said positively. "I saw a man. And he chased me.—You're not very hospitable here!"

The woman's head came up. "No, we are not," she agreed in her monotonous tone. "You better go now." Footsteps sounded—first overhead, then coming down the stairs. The dull expression faded somewhat from the old face. One of the thick, toil-worn hands grasped Judy's arm. "You go now," she said.

Judy stood where she was. "But I *must* see Frederica Hammond," she protested. "I'm not going to leave until I do. If you won't tell me where to find her, I'll find her myself!"

Her own burst of energy surprised her, as did the older woman's reaction. It developed to a vaguely pleading quality.

"Please," she said, lowering her voice, as though begging Judy to do likewise. "Please, you go now. You'll make trouble, if you don't."

"I came to see Frederica," Judy repeated stubbornly. "And I won't go until I have seen her."

"Well," said a quiet voice from the stairs, "here I am."

Judy whirled swiftly to face the girl who stood slightly above them. She was taller than Judy had pictured her, but very slender. Golden hair, falling to her shoulders, framed the fine features, rather narrow deep blue eyes, a short straight nose, a mouth that was soft—and yet stubborn. She wore an ankle-length, pale blue dressing gown, full-sleeved, gathered at the waist under a wide white sash. But it was the girl's cheeks that held Judy's attention, the color of her complexion. Pale and drawn, she appeared, and her hands, against the wood of the doorway, were long fingered and far too thin for real beauty.

Judy experienced a strange sensation of having seen Frederica Hammond before, of having met her. But then, she already knew so much about the girl, that she might be the victim of an hallucination.

Frederica Hammond, however, was swift to recognize Judy, and utter amazement came over the pale face. "Miss—Garland!" She came down the steps. "What are *you*—of all people—doing here?"

The name meant nothing to the older woman. She said stodgily, "She came in without being asked and she won't go away. Mr. Frazer—"

"It's all right, Elizabeth," Frederica said. She smiled faintly at Judy. "It must be all right, I'm sure. But—I don't understand."

Judy said swiftly, "It won't take you long to understand. If we can have just a moment—alone."

Judy reflected afterward that she might have given Frederica the Doyles' message then and there. She might have thrust the package into Frederica's hand, saying, "Mrs. Brit wanted you to have it back. She was worried about the way it turned up in her shop." Then Judy might have rushed out again, away from this quiet, forbidding place, where a Mr. Frazer seemed master of everyone's fate.

But, even if she had done this and hurried away, still her stay at the Mattis house was inevitable. She was a victim of circumstances, caught in a trap so cleverly woven that she did not realize that it was a trap at all.

Frederica, for all her frail appearance, had an active mind. She said quickly and quietly, "Elizabeth, I wish you would please bring up a pitcher of chocolate. Hot and not too sweet. And something salty, wafers or toast. Will you?"

"Yes, but—"

Frederica had her hand on Judy's arm. "We're going up to my room."

Elizabeth's green eyes came to life.

"But, Miss Freddy!" she protested. "Mr. Frazer said—"

"He's in the library. He hasn't heard us. And even if he has—?" Frederica's eyes went beyond the short flight of stairs, and for a moment she listened. "No," she decided, "he hasn't found out that anyone's here, or he would have come." Her hand on Judy's arm was urging her to follow, quickly.

"We'll go up to my room," she repeated in a guarded voice. "I don't think he'll hear us. I'm sure of it. The stairs are thickly padded."

Judy simply nodded. They went, side by side, up the short flight, came to a landing. A life-size oil painting hung there, but it was in such a vague light that Judy could not see it clearly, except to perceive that it depicted a boy and a girl dancing. Frederica paused for the fraction of a moment on the landing, then whispered to Judy, "Hurry!"

They went on up together, for the stairs were unusually wide. Judy was to learn more about the wide stairs in the Mattis house. Now she gave them small thought. It was that urgent, small word, "Hurry!" that gripped at her, tightening her throat.

From the kitchen, standing above Judy and Elizabeth on the stairs, Frederica had looked composed enough. But Judy knew for a certainty that this was far from the truth. The girl was in a state of high, nervous tension. She seemed to fear that they might be followed, despite her saying it would be all right for Judy to come up. She seemed to expect that someone would come after them now—perhaps the Mr. Frazer of old Elizabeth's worried singsong.

They reached the top of the stairs, and Frederica cast one swift, anxious look back down. No one was there and there was no sound in the kitchen, save the movements of Elizabeth. A rattle of pans, the scrape of a spoon, attested that she had begun the preparation of the hot chocolate which Frederica had requested.

"It's all right," Frederica said, scarcely above a whisper. "This way, down the hall, to the left."

It was more like a good-sized room than a hall. Against one wall, Judy spied a chest, which also served as a seat. Above it were rows of bookcases. She found that she had been right about the walls, as she had glimpsed them from the outside. They were the color of mahogany, gleaming darkly under yellow-orange wall lamps.

Frederica turned away from the chest, toward the left. Judy saw one door that was closed, another, next to it, partly open. Toward this latter door Frederica went, motioning Judy to follow. They went inside, and Frederica shut the door. There came the click of a key turning in the lock and then the golden girl gave a sigh that only partly concealed a pitiful little groan.

She said, from the depths of her heart, "Oh, I'm so glad you're here!"

Judy hoped that her smile was reassuring, for she could scarcely add, "I'm glad I'm here, too." No one could enjoy the sort of welcome she had been given at the Mattis house! But Frederica seemed to expect no answer. She went past Judy, toward a heavy, round table where a frilled lamp stood. She motioned to a low rocking chair with a curved back.

Seating herself, Judy studied the room. The light, uncertain wallpaper, the windows with their drawn blinds, heavy lace curtains. Four dark fingers poking upward were the bed. It had a heavily tufted spread on it, white and trailing to the faded, flowered carpet. The dresser was high and carved, with little shelves on either side of it. Heavy silver gleamed in the brush and comb set and in the various trinket boxes.

Frederica took another chair, straight-backed, padded and almost covered with a thick, knitted doily. She brought the chair close to where Judy was sitting.

"Now—," she began, and took a deep breath. "No, take off your coat first. And your hat."

"I—," Judy began, about to say that she could stay only a few moments, but she added, "All right," and slipped out of the coat. She put the little hat on the table, along with the package.

Now she was actually talking to Frederica Hammond. Now was the time to say briefly, "Here's the satin gown you left at Brit's. That's why I came—to give it to you."

But Frederica was talking. "I can't imagine why you've come here, Miss Garland—why you were asking Elizabeth to see me. But I was never so glad to see *anyone* in all my life. I—," she broke off, looked about her, "I feel as though I were living in a kind of dream. As though this weren't—ME!" Her blue eyes pleaded. "Did you ever feel like that?"

Judy nodded. She felt exactly like that right now!

Frederica urged, "Now, tell me. Did I hear you say something about the Doyles?"

"Yes. They—rather, Grace, asked me to come here. She wanted me to tell you they were—" Judy hesitated, about to say "worried." She changed it before the wide gaze of the blue eyes. "They're wondering when you're coming back. They miss you very much."

Frederica bit her lip. "I miss them, too," she said, and looked down at her long fingers, clasped in her lap. Her eyes came up swiftly to Judy's face. "But how did you—a famous movie star—happen to come there, to the Doyles? Or are you a friend of theirs? They never told me."

It was funny, Judy thought. It was strange and wrong and all out of key. She was being questioned, but she had entered this house with the full intention of asking Frederica the questions!

The minutes were flying, she reminded herself. She ought to be starting back to the bus stop, back past the urns where the threatening figure had been lurking. She felt a momentary desire to tell Frederica about that queer little episode, but brushed it aside.

"I'll make my story as short as possible," she said. "I came to bring back something—something you left at a costume shop."

"At a costume shop?" Frederica seemed at a loss. Then she remembered. "Oh. You mean—the white gown?" Her eyes were deeply puzzled. "But I don't see how? I mean, how did you happen to bring it? Or how you *knew*—?"

"It's rather involved," Judy admitted. "I delivered a gift to Dora Brit from her sister. Mrs. Brit was showing me some of her costumes when she came across the gown." Involuntarily, Judy's eyes went to the package on the table. Frederica's eyes followed. Hastily, Judy went on, "Mrs. Brit was worried about having such a costly gown there in the shop. Her son doesn't want her to keep on working, I guess, and she thought—"

Frederica nodded. "I think I understand. She thought it might look as if it had been stolen. But it wasn't."

Judy believed Frederica—yes, this was the truth. The satin gown, the lovely, glowing garment which had brought her here to this strange, too-quiet house, which had made her feel in these few moments that

Frederica Hammond was a girl whom she would never forget, this satin gown was not the kind of contraband Mrs. Brit had feared.

But what was it, then?

For Frederica asked, "How did Mrs. Brit know I had brought it there?"

"Because of the little Dutch doll."

Frederica nodded slowly. "Yes, that's true. I bought the doll and gave my name and address." A fleeting smile lurked at the corners of her mouth. "Mrs. Brit said she had to know where her dolls went." She looked directly at Judy.

"I did so want the doll," she admitted. "I loved it the moment I saw it. And lots of the others, too, but I got that one mostly because I wanted her to leave the room. I asked her to wrap it very carefully. So when she went away, I put the white dress in the cabinet." The girl looked faintly surprised. "She remembered, I suppose, that it was I who came in with a package, and went out without one?"

Judy nodded. "That's right. For an old lady, she has a good memory."

"Yes. And she was busy, too. A whole flock of little boys came in. I thought she wouldn't notice." Frederica sighed. "Well, and so she found me out and asked you to return it. Didn't she know who you *were*?"

Judy said, "Oh, yes. But if I'd been the Queen of Siam, she'd have done the same thing. She was worried sick for fear its presence there might cause her some trouble!"

"Do you know, that never occurred to me." Frederica's eyes moved toward the door that led to the hall. "It was a gift, you see. Aunt Myrta wanted Dora Brit to have the gown."

Aunt Myrta—that must be Mrs. Mattis. But why didn't she give it to Dora Brit openly?

The explanation was quickly forthcoming.

"Aunt Myrta didn't want any of—of *them* to know," Frederica went on, painfully selecting her words. "She asked me to try and leave it there, without anyone knowing. They might—misunderstand."

"They"—Judy wondered— "Who were *they*?" She must have expressed her thought without words, for Frederica went on, "It's her family. Garth and Cilla and Harris. You don't know them, of course, but, well, Aunt Myrta just wanted it that way. She didn't know Mrs. Brit, but she knew that she had a costume shop, and she wanted the gown to be used again and again. She wanted it to be loved by countless wearers. Do you understand?"

Judy recalled how out of place the beautiful garment had seemed among the cheap, hastily fashioned costumes, and she didn't understand Frederica, but she tried to nod understandingly. Frederica, with uncanny swiftness, seemed to have caught Judy's impression. "You think that was a queer place to leave such a dress, don't you?" she said. "Well, so did I, after I got in there. But that's what Aunt Myrta

They Listened in the Too-Quiet House

wanted, and so I did it." She spread her slender hands. "Now you know."

"Yes," Judy thought, "now I know."

But there were many other things she did not know, could not understand. The air of suspense that hung over the house, that seemed to cramp the girl's movements, weighed her down. They were whispering together here, as though an eavesdropper might be standing close to the door that led to the wide hall.

Judy heard a sound, but not at the door. It came from outside. A car was coming up the driveway.

Frederica went to one of the windows, peered through the blind. "That's Cilla, or Harris," she said, under her breath. "Maybe both of them. Now, we're *all* here!"

Judy stood up suddenly. "I'm afraid I'll have to go," she said. "If I don't I'll miss the bus back. I suppose there won't be many more tonight."

Frederica's brows lifted. "Bus?" she said. "You didn't drive out?"

"No, I took the bus."

"But you can't take it back. The last one went just as I came down to the kitchen!"

Judy said weakly, "It—went?" There was a short silence. "Well, maybe I could call a cab."

Frederica was standing, stiff and still. "You can't, Judy," she said, as one girl would say to another whom she regarded as her trusted friend. "The telephone's disconnected. That's why I couldn't call Grace and Marion. I'm—I'm almost what you'd call—a *prisoner*!"

"Why, I—" Judy faltered.

Frederica touched her on her arm. "I'm sorry," she said fervently. "But I'll be honest and say I'm selfishly glad, too. I—I've felt so alone. So frightened!"

Judy heard the car stop. Voices.

She said suddenly, "There was a man out there when I walked along the driveway. He ran after me. I told Elizabeth, and she said something about a spirit of the lake. Do you know what she was talking about?"

"Yes, I know. It was probably Martin who chased you. He's really harmless, except he's got mixed up with some weird cult. He thinks there's a spirit in the lake. Sometimes I think Elizabeth believes in it, too."

"They must be rather grim," Judy said shakily, "the two of them."

"They're not, really." Frederica was listening to the sound of footsteps below them. "I've known them both since I was a child." Lightly, she stepped to the door, pausing in a listening attitude. Her mouth drew into a thin line. "There are some others I'm a lot more worried about," she said, "than any spirits in the lake!"

CHAPTER FOUR

MEDICINE FOR MYRTA

For several minutes the Mattis house had been throbbing with sound, and then came a sudden interlude of silence. The voices and sounds of movement at the front of the house, suggesting the arrival of at least two persons, subsided. No longer could Elizabeth be heard, puttering about in the tiled kitchen. Even the wind, which moaned against the blinds, seemed to be stilled, gathering its forces for a sharper onslaught.

Judy sat stiffly and still in the low rocker, watching Frederica, who pressed herself against the door leading to the hallway. Judy had observed that there were two more doors in this room—one near her, and one at the head of the bed. From behind the door which was closest, Judy thought she had heard a subdued, moaning sound, but she was not certain. In the silence that hung heavily over the strange house, Judy felt caught and helpless, her thoughts in a maddening whirl.

"There are some others I'm a lot more worried about," Frederica's hushed voice seemed to repeat itself in the thick quiet, *"than any spirits in the lake!"*

Did the girl mean those who had come in a short

while ago? Did she mean the Mr. Frazer of whom Elizabeth stood in such profound awe?

Frederica was moving now, her hand on the knob of the door that led into the hall. Turning slightly, she said to Judy, "Elizabeth's coming with the chocolate. Oh, thank heavens!"

The arrival of the chocolate seemed a small blessing to evoke such a deep expression of gratitude, but Judy did not understand, then. She did not understand the nature of the battle in which the valiant girl was engaged, the forces lined against her.

"Just a moment!" Frederica whispered, and darted out into the hall.

Judy heard the faint tinkle of the tray. She sensed, rather than caught, the brief, whispered words that Frederica spoke to Elizabeth. Then the girl was back again in the room, closing the door quietly after her, and, while she held the small tray expertly in one hand, she locked the door with the other.

She came quickly to Judy who had risen.

"I'm going to take this in to Aunt Myrta." Frederica nodded toward the door which was nearest to Judy. "Her room adjoins this."

Judy glanced toward the door. She knew, then, that she really had heard the low moaning sound. Its origin was in this next room.

"Leave the door partly open," Frederica said swiftly. "I don't see how they could suspect that anyone was in here, but I want to make sure. If the door's open—," Frederica paused, listening.

"If the door is open," Judy thought, "they'll be less likely to become suspicious." But she felt a coldness creeping through her. It might be dangerous for her to let her presence become known. Even though her presence in the house would not be discovered, still, it seemed somehow dangerous. There was alarm in Frederica's pale cheeks and wide eyes,—there was warning in the very air they breathed.

"My closet's over there at the head of the bed," Frederica went on, the whispered words spilling from her lips. "Put your things in there, and the package, too, and then turn out the light. You understand?"

Dully, Judy nodded. She felt caught in some desperate situation that had closed upon her like a trap.

"And—*hurry!*" Frederica said, moving closer to the door whence the low moaning sound had come.

The weird sound came now. They both heard it.

"I'll be back—soon," Frederica promised, rather uncertainly, and went out.

She left the door ajar, and for an instant Judy stood as she was. She heard Frederica say, "Here's the chocolate, Aunt Myrta—and buttered crackers," in a tone that would have done justice to any good nurse. Had Judy not seen the other Frederica, the girl with the fear-stricken eyes, she might have been lulled into a false sense of naturalness and well-being, even as the sick woman in the next room was being consoled.

But Frederica was a clever girl. She had donned this mask expertly. Judy lost no time in gathering up her hat and coat, and the package. She sped across the room, put the things into a closet which in spite of the darkness she perceived was astonishingly spacious. Besides the double bar that held the hangers from which dangled Frederica's clothing there was ample room in the closet for a chest of drawers. Judy sensed that the closet ran back farther than her eye could reach, that it extended farther than the garments lined up so neatly beneath the double bar.

The light now—she must turn out the light, she reminded herself.

Her hand found the small knob, turned it. Frederica's room was instantly plunged into darkness. The tall shaft of light coming through the partly opened door to Myrta Mattis's room furnished the only illumination.

Judy felt herself drawn to that light, as a helpless moth is pulled into a candle flame. It was not only the pounding necessity to discover what was happening in this ill-fated household, it was the propelling desire to be near the frail, blond girl. The girl who had said she was a prisoner here. The girl whose destiny had linked itself so closely with Judy's.

Standing flat against the wall, well in the shadow, Judy saw a portion of Myrta Mattis's room. It must be a room of unusual size, running the full width of the house. It *was* the width of the house, as a matter of fact. Judy saw the drapes of faded tapestry at the windows, and she knew that the slits of light she had seen from the bus stop came from here. A desk was within her range of vision. It was wide and low, carved uniquely, and with many shelves. On them were pictures in heavy, silver frames. On either side were cabinets, or perhaps wardrobes. But the bed was not within her view, nor was Frederica, although Judy could hear her talking softly to the woman.

"Are the pillows high enough, Aunt Myrta? There, I think you'd better hold the cup while I hang up this robe."

Judy heard only a murmur from, she assumed, the woman in the bed. The murmur seemed to protest that she was too weak to hold the cup or do anything. But Frederica's voice was gently firm.

"You're so much better. Your color's better, and your eyes are so bright. Pretty soon you'll be up and around again."

Judy caught a glimpse through the open door of the girl moving toward the desk—no, to the wardrobe. She held up a beautiful garment of deep blue with paler blue flowers trailing gently in every direction.

"I'll be so glad when you can come downstairs, wearing this robe," Frederica said, smiling in the direction of the woman in the bed. "The way you're gaining, it'll be no time at all!"

Myrta Mattis sighed—Judy heard her—but it was not a heavy sound. Rather it was a sound of hopeful anticipation. And there came the click of a cup being placed upon a saucer.

Frederica had managed to show the woman that she was perfectly able to sit up and take her own chocolate. And Judy somehow guessed that this was a small victory for the girl. As Frederica turned, after closing the wardrobe, Judy caught the expression on her face. And she knew the girl's expression meant joyous elation.

But it was a short-lived joy. There came the sound of footsteps, and the girl seemed to stiffen, to brace herself.

Myrta Mattis said, "That must be Garth." Her voice was tired. "And Cilla and Harris. I thought I heard them come in."

Frederica appeared outwardly calm, but Judy saw her hands. She was holding them stiffly at her sides, clenched, the nails no doubt biting into the palms. The girl was fighting for control, preparing herself for something she feared, even hated.

And she succeeded admirably. Judy felt a rush of appreciation at the matter-of-fact cheer in her voice when she said, "They'll be glad to find you looking so well, Aunt Myrta. Not needing to take those sleeping pills any more." And Frederica moved away, evidently toward the bed. "I'll pour you another cup."

"You'd better help me." Myrta Mattis's voice

seemed weaker, almost piteous. "My hand is shaking so."

"My hands do that sometimes, too," Frederica said confidingly. "When I'm tired. After I've been drawing a lot." The footsteps were now in the wide hallway, outside the door. "There," Frederica said, almost gaily, "you've finished the second cup. That means sweet dreams for sure!"

But Frederica was far from gay. Myrta Mattis might be lulled into a feeling of well-being, but Judy was not fooled. Frederica was desperately worried, keyed to the inevitable coming of the people who must be a part of this household. Who were they, Judy wondered. Myrta Mattis knew them by their voices and by their footsteps. They must be close to her, emotionally. It could not be said the woman was *afraid*.

Judy stood rooted to the spot, waiting for their entrance. Her own precarious position was out of her thought entirely. She seemed lost in the conflict that raged for the blond girl.

As though trespassing against a "Do Not Disturb" sign, the three came into the room. Judy could not see them at once, but there was in the air that unnamable hush with which visitors approach the bedside of one who is desperately ill. They came as well-wishers who accept the hopelessness of a pitiful situation.

A man spoke first, quietly. His voice seemed deeply considerate. "Myrta, Cilla is here. And Harris."

Frederica said (and Judy knew the effort behind her casualness), "Aunt Myrta heard you come in. She's so glad to see you. Don't you notice how well she looks this evening?"

There was a short pause, as though the girl had spoken with shocking irreverence.

The voice of the man came again, as though he had difficulty in keeping his self-control. "We are glad if you see an improvement, Frederica." The statement was meant to crush her, to tell her that she was misrepresenting an evident truth—that Myrta Mattis looked decidedly as though she had taken a turn for the worse.

Myrta Mattis said fretfully, "Come in. You don't have to stand in the door."

"Yes, Myrta," the man said soothingly, and whispered something to the others.

A woman said, "Well, mother, I finally got here. I'm sorry it took so long, but I had to keep some engagements I couldn't cancel." She must have walked nearer to the bed, Judy thought, for her voice receded. "Don't try to sit up. Lean back."

Myrta Mattis said, "I'm glad—you're here, Cilla. You're looking well." How her voice grew weaker, more uncertain! "And you, too, Harris."

"Thank you." This was a rougher, man's voice. He paused for an awkward instant. "We had a time getting here. It looks like we're in for a blizzard."

Myrta Mattis sighed deeply. "Yes," she said, "a

blizzard." She uttered the words as though she wished she might have the power to rise and watch it from her window, but that even the joy of being out in a snowstorm must be forever denied her, even as everything else of natural beauty had been swept away.

They must be standing in an awkward line, Judy thought. Mourners, crepe-hangers—persons who should be banned by law from any sickroom.

There were quick, light footsteps. Frederica said, "I'll take the tray away, Aunt Myrta." Again, the clink of the dishes, and Frederica saying with determined cheer, "Two whole cups of chocolate. I told her that would surely mean a good sound sleep."

Then Judy saw Garth Frazer. She did not know who he was as he walked toward the desk and leaned against it. She saw the man's back, sideways, the lean shoulders from which a dark coat hung loosely. She saw the black hair tinged with silver, and part of his neck and the side of his face. Wrinkles cut deeply back of the ears and down to the throat. His eyebrows were bushy, his upper lip too long. Judy disliked this man immediately.

"Chocolate?" Judy heard him say. "My dear Freddy, I thought Myrta was to have her sleeping medicine at this time—and a glass of water."

My dear Freddy! Those words were the sleekest sarcasm. The silky syllables covered censure that was like the sharpest dagger underneath a cloak. Frederica was anything but his *dear Freddy,* Judy was sure of that!

"Aunt Myrta's been able to do without the pills for the last three nights," Frederica told him, struggling valiantly to retain her note of cheer. "We thought she'd be able to do without them now."

"*We* thought?" the man repeated, and turned his face so that Judy saw the long, pointed nose, and she noticed the way his hair grew close as a cap on his narrow forehead. "And you permitted this girl to disobey the doctor's orders?" He shot the question at the woman who was ill. "Really, Myrta, how do you ever expect us to help you when you won't cooperate!"

Myrta Mattis said wearily, "Oh, Garth, *don't!* I'm tired!"

Another man now came within Judy's range of vision. Shorter than Garth, he was wearing an overcoat of thick brown wool and a felt hat back on his head. Judy noticed his eyebrows, thick, raised now in a look of surprise, and his blunt nose, square jaw. In one hand he held a pipe, like a kind of excuse, as though he wished he might make haste in getting away from this place of sickness to enjoy it. The free hand he put on Garth's shoulder. The others in the room could not see this, but Judy did. The square-jawed man was tapping meaningfully on Garth's lean shoulder.

"I better put the car away," he said. "Looks like we'll have some shoveling out to do in the morning."

Frederica said, "Oh, are you staying tonight?"

"Why, yes." The speaker was the daughter whom Judy had not seen. She spoke as though she were smiling, but with eyes that were colder than the wind that rattled at the windows. "Should we have told you, Freddy?"

"I didn't mean that, Cilla," Frederica said quickly, huskily. "I'm sure your mother is very glad to have you with her."

"Indeed?" Cilla said bitingly. Her voice lowered. "And take your job away from you, my dear?"

"I don't need anybody's job, Cilla!"

Myrta Mattis cried woefully, "Can't you stop that bickering? You're making me worse! Can't you see I'm sick—*sick*?"

Frederica said, swiftly contrite, "Oh, Aunt Myrta, I'm sorry! We'll go and leave you. So you can rest."

"Yes," Garth said, rising from the desk. His back was toward Judy. She saw his long, powerful fingers clasped together behind him. "I hope you can, Myrta, without the medicine the doctor prescribed for you." He turned to Harris. "I'll go with you."

The two moved out of Judy's line of vision. Garth said, farther away, "I'll see you in the morning, Myrta. I hope you sleep well."

Harris said uneasily, "Well, good night, Myrta."

Myrta Mattis responded drearily, "Good night—good night," and the two went out the door. But Judy did not hear the daughter, Cilla, leaving. She was moving about, however—or was it Frederica? Judy decided it was the daughter, for presently she spoke: "You still keep these old pictures, mother. Weren't we funny-looking then?"

Myrta Mattis said, "They aren't funny to me," in a defensive tone, sturdier than before. "Good night, Cilla. Come and see me in the morning."

Clearly this last speech was dismissal, and the daughter resented it. "All right, mother," she said with a hint of amusement in her tone, wholly out of key. "I *am* tired. I've been so busy. It was quite an effort getting here." She moved toward the hallway door. "I hope you sleep well."

Judy thought, "She's mean. Downright nasty!" But Cilla had not finished. She said, as though recalling a trifle that had escaped her attention briefly, "Oh, Freddy, could I see you for a moment?"

Judy woke to her precarious situation. If this so-busy daughter wished to speak to Frederica confidentially, it might be *here*, in this very room. It was not likely that Cilla would go back downstairs.

Frederica must have been taken by surprise, too, but her composure was admirable. Admirable, too, was the way she warned Judy.

"*Now*?" she said, with mild interest. "In my room?"

"Why not?" said Cilla.

"Indeed." The word sounded as if Frederica shrugged. "Why *not*?"

Myrta Mattis said something, perhaps requested that Frederica return, but Judy did not wait to listen further. The light from the open door was enough to show Judy the way to the clothes closet. and when the two came to the door that led to Frederica's room from the hallway, Judy was safely hidden back of the rows of garments in the closet. In her haste, she had not closed the closet door firmly, but she could not risk moving about now, lest she betray her hiding place.

Cilla said in the hallway, "This door's locked," and Frederica replied, "Why, yes, I remember now, I did lock it. But we can go in the other door."

"I might have had time," Judy thought, "to close the closet door—but I'll stay where I am. After all, how could anyone know I'm in here!"

Then she remembered Martin. If, as Frederica thought, the man who had leaped from the shadow of the heavy urn, *was* Martin, he would know that she had come in, wouldn't he? Perhaps he had already told Garth and the others. Perhaps that was what Cilla wanted to talk about!

Judy suffered a moment of panic—her heart beat so loudly that it surely must betray her! Valiantly stifling her excitement, Judy struggled to regain her composure. The chest was a big thing, and she was crouched behind it. She reassured herself that, even if Cilla did open the closet door, it was not likely that she could be seen.

At any rate, there was only one thing to do: wait.

Frederica said, "I'll be back in a little while, Aunt

Myrta," and she and Cilla came nearer. The lamp on the table was lighted. The glow was a faint pencil of light under the crack of the closet door. This time, Judy would see nothing of what went on, but she would be able to hear all that was said.

A door was closed. The one leading to Myrta Mattis's room, Judy decided. And for a moment, all was quiet.

Frederica's voice said, "Well, what is it, Cilla?"

"I was just wondering," slowly, too thoughtfully, came the other's reply, "what you expect to get by your little Florence Nightingale performance."

"Yes?"

"Yes. It isn't smart to disobey a doctor's orders."

Frederica said hotly, "Are you sure I'm disobeying orders, Cilla? Have you talked to the doctor?"

"I've talked to Garth," Cilla insisted. "But, somehow, I didn't believe it. Not until I saw how it was with my own eyes."

"Not until you saw what?" Frederica demanded. "That I've been trying to bring a little real comfort into your mother's life, help her to get well? What do *you* know of her illness? How many hours have *you* spent at her bedside?"

"My dear Freddy, you don't seem to realize that I'm a busy woman."

Frederica made a noise that indicated a healthy young skepticism. "I know how busy you are! Standing up before this and that bunch of flag-wavers.

Telling them how to make this a better world!"

"Really, Freddy!" Cilla began angrily, and then she laughed. "You haven't changed much, have you? That same little urchin who used to be thrust on us every summer without being invited. The pictures in mother's room brought it all back so clearly—and now, this!"

"Thrust on you, is right," Frederica said, "but not because *I wanted* to spend my summers here. You were always reminding me that I was a poor relation, Cilla. Wearing your cast-off dresses. Watching you preen yourself. Taking the blame for the mean little things you did."

"Well," Cilla gasped. "Really!"

"Yes, *really*!" Frederica said, and Judy, listening wide-eyed, smiled despite the thick gloom that hung over her head. She thought, "Good for little Freddy! Oh, I wish I could see her face this minute!"

"But you're wrong about one thing," Frederica went on. "I have changed. A lot. I don't have to wear your cast-offs any more. In fact, it might interest you to know that I design my own clothes. And that nifty little three-color number you're wearing right now is one that I dreamed up!"

Cilla laughed. Rather, a laugh began in her throat, but died shortly. Truth was in Frederica's voice, and Myrta Mattis's daughter changed the subject abruptly.

"All right," her voice seemed to snap, "and what

"Thrust on You Is Right," Frederica Said

about your being here? What do you expect to get out of it?"

"Nothing," Frederica said shortly. "I wish I could leave."

"Well, what's keeping you?"

"Ask my jailer, Garth Frazer."

Cilla seemed to sneer vocally. "Yes, I know. I foresaw that you'd say that. Garth won't let you go, you claim—he's holding you here against your will. He told me you'd say that!"

At that moment Frederica's defenses must have crumpled somewhat. There was a small silence, in which Judy strained to hear what was being said. What answer would Frederica make?

The blond girl's voice came at last, wearily. "It's no use, Cilla. You've built up something hateful and mean. You want to believe Garth, so—go ahead and believe him! But one thing you can't make me do. You can't make me stand by idly and see harm come to Aunt Myrta!"

"Of all things!" Cilla gasped. "As though Garth would do anything to harm his own sister!"

"Myrta's not his sister. They're not blood relations at all. As you know very well!"

"But I am a blood relation," Cilla said silkily. "And so are you, dear Freddy. But please remember, mine is a greater claim. If anything happens to mother—"

"Nothing's going to happen to your mother. Not if I can help it!"

There was a slight movement.

"I give you credit," Cilla said smoothly. "You *have* changed, Freddy. It'll be more fun than ever, getting the best of you!" The woman must have moved toward the door. Judy heard the key turning in the lock. "I'll see you in the morning," Cilla said. The door opened and closed.

To Judy's ears came the sound of muffled sobs.

Frederica—no, Freddy, for that was the way Judy thought of the "golden" girl—Freddy must be too crushed by the hateful attack to come to the closet and tell her the way was clear. Judy herself felt a great weariness, as though she had run a desperate obstacle race, and had suddenly come up against a hurdle too great to overcome.

The sobs continued until Judy could endure the waiting no longer. She crept out from behind the chest, stealthily opened the closet door. Freddy was sitting hunched forward in the rocking chair, her face buried in her hands. Judy went to her quietly, put a hand on the quivering shoulder.

"Don't, Freddy," she said. "She's not worth it!"

"Oh, Judy!" Freddy's hand caught hers. "They're so—so horrible!" A tear-stained face lifted. "How *could* she believe such a thing? How *could* she think that I—!" Freddy broke off. "But it's Garth Frazer. He's turning them all against me. Making them think that I—"

Judy knelt beside her.

"I know," Judy soothed. Her hand went over the shining head. "But you can't give in like this, Freddy. You have to fight back, don't you see?"

The sobs had quieted.

"Garth is trying to make it look as though I don't want Aunt Myrta to get well. Do you see how clever he is, Judy? He pretends to be so worried over her, and he makes everything worse. And those sleeping pills!"

"Did the doctor really prescribe them?" Judy's hand continued its gentle motion. "I heard it all, Freddy. Everything. And I'm willing to bet a doctor hasn't seen Mrs. Mattis in a long time."

"You're right! As far as I know, it's been Garth who has talked to the doctor. I don't even know *which* doctor. There's no name, nothing, on the box of pills Garth says she is supposed to take." Freddy's hands caught at Judy's arm, holding it in a grip almost too keen for comfort. "But, Judy, suppose it were right? I mean, suppose a doctor did really prescribe the medicine. I don't truthfully know, you see. It's just—what I feel, that Aunt Myrta shouldn't have them!"

Judy's thoughts raced. "Listen, Freddy, does Garth ever give her the medicine?"

"Why, no. No, he doesn't."

"Who does?" Judy persisted, driven by an idea of her own.

"Well, Elizabeth. Or Aunt Myrta takes the pills herself."

"You mean that Garth only suggests it. Makes her ask for them, or want them."

Freddy nodded. "That's right." She brightened. "So I must be on the right track. He *wants* her to have them, but he won't have any part in the business of seeing that she does take them. Oh, he's clever!"

"So I gather," Judy agreed. "Building up the idea of how sick she is, while he pretends to be all gentle concern!"

"That's exactly it!" Freddy regained much of her spirit. "And he won't let me get away, because—" Freddy broke off, shuddering.

Because, Judy guessed, he wants to put all possible blame for anything that might happen upon Freddy's innocent shoulders!

The two were quiet, each busy with her own thoughts. Presently, Freddy got to her feet. Judy stood watching while the girl paced the length of the room.

"Oh, Judy," she said bleakly, "what *am* I to do!" The blue eyes widened with the weight of a sudden realization. "And—what about *you*? You're in this now, too. This horrible mix-up! And it's all my fault—I shouldn't have brought you up here! But I was so—so afraid!"

"Don't worry about me," Judy tried to say staunchly. "There's a way out. If we just work together, we can find it!"

But what was the way out? Freddy had not been

able to find one. Freddy, who knew the house, knew the people.

The wind was howling outside, pressing at the blinds, hemming them in, all of them. Judy felt as though a trap were closing in on her, holding her helpless, at the mercy of Garth Frazer. A mad man. Mad with greed, at any rate. Surely, not sane.

A soft knock came at the door. Freddy stared at it. "Wait," she told Judy, and sped across the room.

CHAPTER FIVE

A WAY OUT?

Freddy had not locked the door after Cilla had gone out. That was the thought that burned in Judy's mind at the moment. Anyone might have opened it slightly, might have been standing there in the hallway, listening to what they had said. And now whoever it was out there was making his presence known, coming to demand that Judy explain *her* presence in Frederica's room.

The blond girl had almost reached the door. She said softly, "Just a moment," and turned to wave a frantic hand at Judy, urging her to disappear again into the clothes closet.

Judy had already opened the closet door. The next moment, she was again inside, but not behind the chest, near the line of clothing. There would not be time now for her to go farther back in the small room. And seconds counted, for Freddy was admitting someone.

No sound of surprise came from the girl, however. Judy heard a low murmur and the door closed. This time, Freddy locked it. The voices came softly, Freddy's and another's, and the closet door was suddenly opened.

"It's all right, Judy," Freddy said. "It's only Elizabeth. When I took the tray, I asked her to come up as soon as she could."

"I couldn't come sooner," the serving woman said. "I was busy fixing up their beds." She spoke in a monotone, but seeing her for the second time, Judy knew the woman better. She sensed a resentment toward the arrivals of the evening.

Freddy asked the woman, "Where did you put them, Elizabeth?"

"Miss Cilla's in the East Room, and Mr. Harris is in the Big South with Mr. Frazer."

Not knowing the plan of the house, Judy benefited little by this information. But the mention of the name Harris made her curious. In their little talk, Freddy had not mentioned Harris. Despite the urgency of the moment, Judy asked swiftly, "Who is he, Freddy? Harris, I mean?"

"He's my cousin, Harris Morley. On the other side of the family. Aunt Myrta's sister was my mother."

Judy said, "I see." But she did not miss the look in Elizabeth's pale eyes. It suggested rebellion.

"What'd he come here for anyway?" she asked Freddy.

"I think Garth asked him to," Freddy said. "I think Garth asked them both to come."

Elizabeth shrugged, as though accepting the added burden stoically.

"Mr. Frazer wanted Mr. Harris in the Big South

with him. They're talking in there," Elizabeth offered. She crossed her arms, waiting.

But Freddy had to talk quickly with the old servant. She did not need the reminder.

"Did Martin see Miss Garland come in?" Freddy asked.

"Sure he saw her."

"I mean," Freddy's hands moved impatiently as she spoke, "did he know it was she—a girl? Or did he think it was the spirit of the lake?"

"He thought it was the spirit."

"*He thought it was the spirit*," Freddy repeated. "You're sure of that, Elizabeth?"

The woman nodded. "I'm sure. He came in and told me, but I was busy making the chocolate."

"Did he know that anyone came in the back door?" Freddy persisted.

"She ran so fast, he wasn't sure. He thought she, the spirit, I mean, went on past the house."

Freddy drew a deep sigh, and Judy felt her own nerves relax their tension.

"And you're sure you didn't talk to him about it, Elizabeth?" Freddy went on. "You didn't tell him anybody came to see me?"

"No, I didn't."

"Or Garth—Mr. Frazer? You didn't tell *him*?"

Elizabeth shook her head. "There wasn't time. Miss Cilla and Mr. Harris came. I was busy getting the chocolate."

"Oh, I'm so glad!" Freddy said fervently. She went close to the old woman. "Elizabeth, I want you to do something for me. *Don't* tell Mr. Frazer!"

"But—!"

"And *don't* tell Martin. I mean, don't tell him anything *about a girl.* Tell him you think there was a spirit, too. Say that you saw something you never saw before." Her head turned briefly toward Judy. "That's the truth, you never saw her before, did you?"

"No." The old head wagged a negative. "I never did." The green eyes narrowed, forcing newer wrinkles in the dried cheeks. "Why should I tell him about the spirit?"

"Because it'll help me, Elizabeth. And it'll help Aunt Myrta. Please believe me. You've got to believe me!"

The woman looked down at her slippered feet, toeing in. Her lips moved, but she said nothing.

"Mr. Frazer will never hold it against you," Freddy went on, "because he'll never know. Miss Garland will leave soon, and everything will be all right. Please, Elizabeth. If you won't do it for my sake, do it for my mother's!"

The old lips worked pitifully. The old head nodded in agreement but with reluctance.

"When you put it that way, Miss Freddy, there's nothing more I can say. There never was anybody like your mother." A hand came up, brushing away a tear. "But you won't ask me for the shoes or the clothes, will you?"

"No," Freddy promised. "I won't ask you about those. Just don't let anybody know she's here!"

"I'll keep it," Elizabeth said, "to myself."

Freddy's hand was on her shoulder, patting it. The old woman turned, went her shuffling way to the door. Freddy opened it and then locked it after her.

Judy picked a question from the puzzled jumble of her thoughts and voiced it: "What did she mean by *shoes* and *clothes,* Freddy?"

The pale girl smiled faintly. "Mine—my shoes and my clothes. Garth had her take them away. About all I have to wear is this robe." She lifted the light folds. "And these slippers." They were fragile things, silver straps crossing the ankles. "Garth," Freddy explained grimly, "didn't want me to run away."

Judy let her eyes glance over at the clothes closet. "But all those things in there?" she said. "What are they?"

"Costumes," Freddy said. "Costumes Aunt Myrta used to wear when she sang."

They heard the voice in the next room calling, "Freddy?"

"She's finished looking at the book I left with her," Freddy explained swiftly. "I'm glad they didn't take that away! Just a minute, Judy, while I look in. I'll be right back."

Judy waited while the girl went in to Myrta Mattis's room, while they talked briefly, the girl's voice gentle and kind, the woman's less fretful than when the others had been there.

Presently, Freddy returned. "I'll have to go back after a while and tuck her in," she said. "She wants to read a little longer. I had to move the lamp for her."

Judy heard this explanation with a divided interest. She was thinking about Garth Frazer, about his taking, or having Elizabeth take, Freddy's clothing. "Did he think he could keep you here by taking your shoes and clothes?" Judy asked.

Freddy rose to meet the challenge in Judy's voice. "*He* thinks so," Freddy admitted. "Garth has so much personal pride that he'd never believe that anyone would rush out to the highway in this get-up—or in one of Aunt Myrta's fancy costumes." The girl's eyes narrowed. "But I'd do it, even if the snow was over my head—if I really wanted to." She seemed to wilt a little. "You see, I don't really want to. I couldn't ever leave *her*." The blue eyes went toward Myrta Mattis's adjoining room. "Not the way things are now."

Judy nodded. "And I suppose Martin is a kind of guard."'

"Part watch-dog," Freddy admitted. "He'd report it if he saw me trying to run away. I don't know what Garth would do then." The frail shoulders trembled slightly. "But I'm not trying to run away. First, I'll build up Aunt Myrta's strength. And then—"

They had seated themselves side by side on the

bed. Judy could see their two heads, close together, reflected in the mirror over the dresser, the thick, dark hair, and the golden halo. Several hours ago, Judy had not known that this girl existed. Nor this lonely house with its strange occupants. It seemed as though she moved in some kind of haze or dream from which she must soon and suddenly awaken.

She looked away from the mirror, toward the windows, three of them, along the wall behind the round table and the two chairs. That was North, Judy thought. The front of the house was West. It was past the front of the house the bus had come.

And her rambling thoughts ceased there, drawn abruptly to center upon her coming here.

"Freddy!"

"What's the matter?" Startled by the fear in Judy's eyes, the blond girl looked quickly about the room. "Did you see—?"

"No. I was thinking about the bus."

"The bus?" Freddy repeated, puzzled.

"Yes. Do you think Martin saw me getting off? He was hiding near one of the urns on the porch, the one farthest away from the driveway."

A frown creased Freddy's forehead.

"I don't think he saw you," she said slowly. "No. I'm sure he didn't. He told Elizabeth he saw the *spirit*."

"But the bus stopped," Judy persisted. "And I got off—"

"The bus always stops there before it makes the turn to the right. It's a bad corner. There's that big cluster of trees." Freddy bit her lower lip. "No, I'm sure he couldn't have seen you. Not until you came nearer the driveway."

The sight of the highway and the thick trees was blotted out by the drawn blinds, but the picture was engraved on Judy's memory. The snow, the house ahead, the great urns, and the figure that had lurked near one of them—she pictured the entire scene. In spite of herself, she shuddered. "I—I'm glad I can run," she said shakily, masking her nervous state.

But Freddy was not fooled.

"He *must* have given you a scare," she said in warm sympathy. "But we don't have to worry about Martin. Elizabeth'll see to it that he keeps on believing he saw his spirit." It was Freddy's turn to laugh weakly. "Martin's ghost talk was kind of a nuisance, but I'm glad of it now."

A little silence settled between them, not awkward, but rather bringing them closer together—two girls in a predicament if ever there was one.

A way out, Judy had promised Freddy. There *must* be a way out.

The thought came, ruefully—the only way had been *in*! Arriving in a snowstorm, with a lovely satin gown, being mistaken for a ghost—that was the way Judy got into the Mattis house. The way *out* was another matter.

Because, even though Freddy were held here, she, Judy must leave—if for no other reason than to bring help to the frightened girl. What help she might bring, Judy did not decide. First, she must make her escape.

That meant breaking through the snow, which must be of considerable depth if it had continued to fall as before. It meant getting through to the highway and hailing a bus or a passing car. But, more than that, it meant eluding the watchful eye of Martin. *Enter, spirit,* Judy's thoughts ran foolishly, *but exit*—?

She brushed the thick curls back from her face.

Freddy gave a small sigh. "Now what?" she said.

"I've got to get away from here," Judy told her firmly.

Freddy's eyes widened. One long, thin hand clasped Judy's arm. "*Now?*" she said. "But how, I mean—?"

She meant she did not want Judy to go.

"I can't be forever darting into clothes closets," Judy said, managing a smile. "I wouldn't be of much help to you that way."

"I know, but—"

"So," Judy went on, forcing a lightness she was far from feeling, "I'll have to make the break for freedom, you know—so as not to be a prisoner here."

Freddy came quickly, but without a sound, to her feet. She went to the dresser, ran her fingers through her hair. Her eyes fell upon the door to Myrta Mattis's room and she went closer to it, listening. All was quiet. She came back to Judy.

"You're right," she said. "You have to go. I was selfish in wanting you here. What good will it do? Dragging you into my family troubles?"

"Family troubles" was putting it mildly, Judy thought a trifle bitterly.

"I might do some good," Judy promised. "In fact, Freddy, that's exactly why I want to get away. To help you. You can't go on here like this. It's—nerve-racking!"

Freddy seated herself again at Judy's side on the edge of the four-poster bed. Her head was bent downward, resting on the palms of her hands. Through the slim fingers, her voice came woefully, muffled. "My head aches so!"

And Judy, who could not have been as old as Freddy, felt suddenly to have gained in years, and in courage and purpose.

"I'll go back to the Doyles," she said. "I'll tell Grace what's happening here. She'll know what to do. And she'll do it, Freddy. Everything will come out all right—you just wait and see!"

The golden head lifted. "Yes," Freddy said. "Grace would know what to do." Her eyes clouded again. "But how can you get away, Judy?"

"I don't know," Judy admitted. "You'll have to put on your thinking cap, Freddy. It's Martin I'm worried about."

Freddy Sat Down on the Bed Beside Judy

"Yes," Freddy said. "Martin."

"Where does he live? In the house?"

"No. Back in the garage. It's enormous. He and Elizabeth have the whole second floor. But they only use three of the rooms."

"The garage," Judy repeated thoughtfully. "That's a help. Do you know what time they go to bed?"

"Well—" Freddy hesitated. "They're usually out of the house by this time. But it's probably later tonight, because Elizabeth was busy getting things ready for Cilla and Harris. But Martin could have gone out there by now."

"Unless," Judy put in, "he's out looking for his spirit of the lake." Her eyes went to the dark windows. "Where *is* the lake, Freddy?"

"Over beyond the main highway. It's northwest of the house. My room and Aunt Myrta's are nearest to it."

"Then, if Martin is still spirit-hunting," Judy said, "he's probably right below us. So crawling down the side of the house would be impossible."

Freddy looked up, in wild protest. "Oh, you never could do *that*! Why, you'd kill yourself, Judy! Besides, it's horribly cold. Listen to that wind!"

"All right," Judy said. "Then how can I get out?"

Freddy's eyes darted to the hallway door. "It'd have to be down the stairs, to the kitchen. But not out the back door. The snow's made everything so bright. Martin or Elizabeth could see you from the garage."

Judy waited throughout a small, panic-filled pause. "Isn't there any other way?" she prodded at last. "Think, Freddy!"

"Oh, I *am* thinking!"

"The storm's getting worse," Judy reminded her. "There won't be many cars passing."

Freddy looked at her, looked past her into space, and then the blue eyes lighted. "I know!" she said softly. "The torture room!"

"The torture room!" Judy breathed in a large gulp of air. She had goaded Freddy into swift thinking, but this was hardly the result she had anticipated. More than ever she thought she must be dreaming, like Alice in Wonderland.

"It sounds awful," Freddy admitted, "but it isn't. The torture room is just a room in the basement, a part of the basement, really. Cilla called it that, when we were children here." Freddy's eyes went back through the years. "For a long time, I didn't know about it, or the way to get there. We used to play hide-and-seek. And I never could find Cilla. She would disappear like magic. The house is filled with all kinds of built-in chests and cabinets. Even secret panels. There's one back of one of the shelves in the dining-room. I knew about most of them, but I did not know of the door under the kitchen stairs." She looked directly into Judy's deeply interested eyes. "You know where the little stairs go up to the main stairway?"

"Where you were standing when I first saw you?"

"Yes. Well, under there is a door. It leads down to a kind of a little basement, apart from the rest of the house. I finally caught Cilla going into it once. I'll never forget how angry she was!"

Judy found the recital interesting enough, but the wind seemed to wail a warning to her to hurry, hurry, while there was still time to make her escape. She said, "But how could I get out of there? Out of the basement?"

"There're some steps," Freddy said, "that kind of wind around, till you come to a door. It's just about under the back entrance to the house."

Judy bit her lip thoughtfully. "But—they'd still be able to see me from the garage, wouldn't they?"

"Not if you were crouching down low. Not if you wore something white against the white snow." Freddy's eyes went to the clothes closet. "Aunt Myrta's got so much stuff in there."

"I might wear the satin gown," Judy said, and though she was trying to keep her mind clearly on the need to be confident and to inspire confidence in the girl at her side, her voice sounded grim in her own ears.

I hate that dress, was what Judy thought.

But that was silly. Why hate anything? *Face the facts,* she told herself. *Think. Think! You have to get out of here, no matter how outrageously fantastic the way may be. No matter if you have to go crawling through the snow like some white animal—or a spirit in the night.*

A spirit!

"Listen, Freddy," she said in a rush, "even if Martin or Elizabeth *should* see me, I could make them think I was their spirit of the lake. I'll wail and moan—and manage somehow. So let's hurry and find something for me to wear."

"Oh, Judy!" Freddy mourned. "This is awful!"

It was rather dreadful and terrifying, but Judy would not let Freddy go on believing it. Nor herself. "Don't you think I could play the spirit part?" she said. "I'll admit it's a little out of my line, but it's a good test to prove my ability."

Words. Words! How uselessly, foolishly, they spilled from her mouth, while she tried not to think too hard of what ordeal might lay before her, while the wind tore at the windows of the lonely old house.

Freddy stood up, no longer able to endure her fears quietly. Judy came to her side.

The two stood, looking into each other's eyes.

"Couldn't you stay, just for tonight?" Freddy begged.

"I could. But what about tomorrow? You'd have to go on hiding me in here. Someone might come barging in—."

"What if they did find you?" Freddy demanded. "You've done nothing you need to be afraid of! After all, look who you are!"

Judy felt the stiff smile tearing at her lips.

Look who she was—that was it. Who she *was.* In some remote past, Judy Garland. But time had roared on its way. Hours by the clock, but it might have been months, years. Time did not count. It was what was around you. The fear that tore at your throat. The horrible, lost feeling of being *out* of time. No, she was only a girl, aghast at the task before her, fighting for the courage to carry it out.

"If I'm going to help you, Freddy, I'll have to get away. *Now!* Don't you see, he might hold me, too. Because—I *know!*"

Freddy's arms went limply to her sides. She realized the truth of what Judy said. Garth Frazer might hold Judy, too.

"But, most of all," Judy went on, "I want to get to Grace Doyle. She's the one who can help you."

Freddy brightened visibly. "Judy! Grace knows you're here! If you aren't back there by tomorrow, she might come, or send someone!"

"No," Judy said slowly, forcing her thoughts back over what had happened. "No, I don't think she expects to hear from me at all. Or, rather, I don't think she'd be particularly disappointed if she didn't. Grace asked me to give you a message, that was all. To tell you they missed you, so you'd come back. If you didn't, right away, she wouldn't be alarmed. They'd go on waiting a while longer. Grace thought I was going to give you a message, and take the next bus back. She never dreamed—"

Judy broke off, leaving the words unsaid. But Freddy felt their heavy import. Who could ever dream that such a hateful thing could actually be going on, under the guise of affectionate concern, in this gaunt old house?

"So," Judy went on, after the brief pause, "we'd better get busy and find my disguise."

It was she who went first to the clothes closet. Freddy remained standing where she was. "I hate to have you do this, Judy," she said, so faintly Judy scarcely caught the words. "It's all my fault—!"

"It's nobody's fault," Judy said flatly. "It's something that happened. It's up to us to do something about it."

But it *was* somebody's fault. It went back to Garth Frazer, the pretender. And something much worse—anger flamed in Judy's heart at the thought of him. Anger made her fingers, moving among the garments in the clothes closet, more swift, more certain.

"Is there a light in here?" she asked Freddy, and succeeded in making her voice matter-of-fact. "It's almost like another room, isn't it?"

Freddy agreed that, yes, it was almost like another room, her voice trailing away into a sigh. But she came to Judy's side, reached in, and pulled a heavy cord. A light over the garments beamed whitely.

"That's more like it," Judy said. And then she saw what type of costumes were hanging here. Nothing like those at Dora Brit's shop. Here was beauty, richness of cloth and trimming. Deep reds, bright blues, pure white. Evening gowns. Of the most extravagant type.

"Well," Judy said slowly, "your Aunt must have been a great performer!"

"Oh, she was!" Freddy said, fervently. Standing beside Judy, looking at the beautiful gowns, the girl seemed more like a person, less like one of Martin's white, worried spirits. "Aunt Myrta sang. The concert stage. She was wonderful! Maybe you think these," her hand going to a luscious green silk, "are kind of gaudy. But they weren't when Aunt Myrta wore them. She was—perfect!"

"I'm sure of it," Judy agreed.

Something touched the toe of one of her shoes and she looked down. There was the package, the fateful white satin dress.

Freddy picked it up, and placed it on top of the chest.

"I wish Mrs. Brit had kept it," Freddy said. "Aunt Myrta wanted others to enjoy it, to be beautiful wearing it."

Because, Judy thought, *the enjoyment of these beautiful things would be denied to her.*

But that must not be. Myrta Mattis must not sink, helplessly, into the pit that yawned at her feet—the cleverly contrived trap of a man who must be absolutely without any decent feelings. Nor must Freddy suffer because of him. Now, before it was too late, Judy must break away, clear the way for them.

"I'll have to wear my fur coat," she planned, while her hands moved over the soft folds. "So it'll have to be something that can be spread out, something that'll come over my head and shoulders at least."

Freddy had accepted the inevitable. "I know what," she said, and pushed her way farther back. "There's a white satin cape here. Just a minute, and I'll find it."

But the cape was not on the racks. It was in one of the drawers in the chest. Freddy found it at last, while Judy stood, fidgeting at the impatience that flamed in her.

"Give it to me, Freddy," she said, taking the cape. They came back into the room, and Judy held it before her. It was wide, generously wide, and long. At first, Judy thought it had a hood. But it was a kind of smaller collar, one that went over the shoulders.

"You could put that up over your head," Freddy said, reading Judy's feminine thought.

"Yes. It will be perfect!" Judy slipped the cape over her shoulders, lifted the collar over her dark curls. "I can pin it under my chin," she said, and looked down. A portion of the green wool dress showed. "It covers me enough to give the illusion." She laughed, because Freddy needed to have her laugh. The girl seemed ready to burst into tears.

Judy said, "There," and laid the cape on the bed. "Now, we'd better listen and see if the house is quiet, if Cilla's gone to bed. Her room is next to this, isn't it?"

"The linen closet is next," Freddy said miserably. "Cilla's is back a little, down a sort of narrow hall. It's—it's hard to explain, unless you could see it."

Judy had no wish to explore the way to Cilla's room. But it was heartening to know that Myrta Mattis's daughter was some little distance away.

"We're almost at the top of the stairs," Judy said, picturing what she had seen. "All I have to do is pass Mrs. Mattis's room. I go down to the landing, where that picture is, and then down to the kitchen." She glanced at Freddy for confirmation.

The blond girl nodded, at a loss for words.

Judy looked about briskly. "Now for my coat. You listen at the door, Freddy. We'll have to make sure no one's in the hall."

But Frederica Hammond never reached the hallway door. From the one which gave onto Myrta Mattis's room came the woman's voice, clear, every word clean cut.

"Freddy," she called, "please come in."

The blond girl gasped something, rushed to the door.

"And," said Myrta, "bring the girl in with you."

Freddy was in the doorway. Judy saw her, a frail statue, staring ahead, unwilling to believe her ears.

Myrta repeated, "Bring her in. I'd like to see her."

Freddy caught her breath, turned to Judy. *She*

knows! Freddy's eyes said; *she knows you're here. You'll have to come in. You can't possibly leave now!*

The white cape was waiting on the four-poster bed. Judy glanced at it once, turned away. Her heart was beating so wildly, it seemed to choke her. One hand went to her throat, as she moved across the room to Freddy's side.

CHAPTER SIX

DUAL PERSONALITY

Freddy was standing close beside her, but it seemed to Judy that the girl's voice came from a distance. She was saying, "Aunt Myrta, this is—a friend of mine."

Myrta Mattis was sitting propped up on pillows in a bed which must have been at least a hundred years old. It was high at the headboard, and its woodwork was carved elaborately with fruits and flowers. Judy saw this fleetingly, for the woman who looked at her dominated the strange, awkward moment. What a beautiful woman she was, Judy thought. Her hair was almost black against the white of the pillows. Her skin glowed a warm olive. The eyes that looked at Judy were heavy-lidded under slim black brows. A straight, delicate nose, lips that were full, the under-lip small with a cleft—she looked like a Greek goddess, if a Greek goddess could be deeply tanned and have the color and the fire that burned in the loveliness of Myrta Mattis.

That was what Judy saw—the fire, the vitality the woman had. Perhaps it was the deep coral of the knitted bed jacket, the careful make-up. But no, it went deeper than that.

Judy heard her own voice, like a shy little girl's: "I'm—I'm sorry you are ill." Even as she said it, she thought, *She doesn't look ill! She looks marvelous. Terribly thin, but marvelous!*

Myrta Mattis smiled, at the two of them. A kind of a twinkle shone in her eyes. She said, to Freddy, "You didn't tell me your guest's name, Freddy."

But she knew, of course, and she was enjoying herself while Freddy gulped, "It's—Garland. Miss Garland."

"How do you do, Judy," Myrta said, as easily and as graciously as though Freddy had told her whom she had been expecting.

Perhaps she knew all along I was in the next room with Freddy, Judy thought. Perhaps she was listening to what we said.

But, no. Myrta was not that type. She was surprised and pleased, but the woman had poise. Judy thought, *How strangely different she looks from the way she sounded before when Garth and the others were in here. And how young she is! I thought she would be old!*

And she had called her Judy!

"I didn't know Freddy knew you," Myrta was saying. She looked at the blond girl who remained close to Judy's side. "You never mentioned it, Freddy."

Freddy managed a laugh. "There're lots of people I haven't had time to mention to you, Aunt Myrta."

"That's true," Myrta said, and to Judy, "Freddy and

I are really getting acquainted. Since she grew up and became a successful business woman, we rather lost track of each other."

"I'm not exactly a business woman," Freddy pointed out.

Myrta looked at her fondly. "You're a wonderful little nurse." She motioned with a beautifully kept hand to a window seat nearer to her bed. "Won't you sit down and have a little visit?"

The girls hesitated. Despite their effort not to look at each other, their eyes drew together. Freddy's thought flashed, "We mustn't! Someone might come to the door. Garth, or Cilla!"

Judy telegraphed back, "We've got to. We'll make it as short as possible."

Myrta misunderstood their reluctance. "You won't tire me," she said, and glanced down at the book on the low table. "I read something this evening that proved wonderfully effective medicine. I really feel better than I have in some time."

Judy moved nearer, and caught at this straw. "Reading can help a lot when you aren't able to be up. I mean, something that gives you a lift."

"Or seeing someone like you coming in unexpectedly," Myrta added. "You, and Freddy, girls with the whole world at your feet!"

It was then the nagging little thought began to grow in Judy's mind. Somewhere, sometime, she had seen Myrta Mattis before. Yet, certainly, she had not heard the name. And it was not an easy one to forget. But that proud, lovely black head—

Myrta smiled as the two seated themselves on the padded window seat. "Now," she said, "you must tell me how you managed to find Freddy 'way out here, and in *such* weather!" Her eyes went over their heads, to the long tapestry drapes. "Just listen to that wind!"

For a short time, Judy had forgotten the wind, but she remembered it now. The wind and the snowstorm. The furious cold that was settling down, heavier and heavier. Here they were sitting, "visiting" as Myrta Mattis had requested, while precious minutes were being lost. She must hurry, hurry away. Get back to the Doyles—tell Grace. Grace would know what to do.

With an effort, she gathered her wildly truant thoughts, made herself respond to the need of the present.

What was it Myrta had asked her? Oh, how she had managed to find Freddy?

"I went to Freddy's apartment," Judy said. "The ladies there told me she was here. I took the bus out."

"The bus?" Myrta's lovely brows lifted. "Are they running in this storm?"

"I—I guess not," Freddy said.

"But," Myrta smiled, "you wouldn't be going back tonight anyhow. You'll stay with us. I hope long enough to get acquainted. I've admired you tremendously, my dear."

"Th-Thank you," Judy said slowly, because the thought persisted that she had seen Myrta Mattis before. And the word "admired" fitted in, too. But too many pieces of the puzzle were missing to fit them together properly, and she was far too tense for real concentration upon any subject but her own escape. The fact that Myrta accepted her so graciously seemed to make it all the worse. It did make it all the worse. Myrta would take it for granted that this was a normal, social call, include all the members of the family in the entertainment of their guest.

And they don't know I'm here! They mustn't know I'm here. Oh, I've got to hurry!

Freddy's hand was on her arm. Freddy knew what she was thinking.

The blond girl said, "Judy's going to bunk in with me tonight, Aunt Myrta. She won't admit it, but she's tired."

Myrta's eyes moved to a tall clock standing at her right, near the door which must lead to the hallway. Judy followed her glance and the hands on the clock told her it was after ten, almost twenty minutes after ten. Less than six hours ago, she had gone to Dora Brit's. Less than six hours ago, she had not known that these people existed.

But she *had* known! Myrta Mattis, *she had known her*. Somewhere. Sometime.

Judy looked away from the clock. She heard Myrta saying that it was getting on to bedtime for girls who

Judy Was Certain She Had Seen Mrs. Mattis Before

must get their beauty sleep, but she was seeing the pictures on the wall, the ones Cilla must have mentioned.

Myrta said, "My rogues' gallery. Cilla and Freddy when they were little." This subject held more for her than dear remembrance. The woman's tone lowered. "When I took a little time to be with them."

Freddy rose to the implied self-criticism. "You were with us as much as you could be Aunt Myrta. We —we had happy summers."

This, Judy guessed, stretched the truth. The summers she had learned about when Cilla and Freddy were talking there in the next room, had been anything but happy. For Freddy, anyhow.

Myrta seemed to go back in her thoughts. "I neglected you," she said, looking at the pictures. "Both you and Cilla. I let you grow away from me."

Freddy came to her feet. She said, with the resumption of her brisk, cheerful-nurse manner, "Well, we're both here now, Aunt Myrta. We'll start making up for lost time."

Myrta's eyes softened, looking at the blond girl. "You're a dear child," she said, and turned suddenly to Judy who had also risen. "You didn't come with Cilla, did you?" she asked. "She didn't say—?"

This was dangerous ground. Judy could *not* say, "I came before they did. I ran in the back door, because a man who was hiding back of one of the urns was chasing me. I had to argue Elizabeth into letting me in. Perhaps I never would have *got* in, if Freddy hadn't discovered me. And hurried me up the stairs, hiding me in her room."

Freddy came to the rescue. "Oh, no. Judy came before them. She's been resting in my room. We—we thought maybe you might be too tired to see her tonight."

Myrta shook her head. "I'd never be too tired to see Judy Garland," she said. It did not mean so much the girl, as all the beauty and depth of the things she had achieved. A bouquet of a speech, but Judy was definitely a girl now, far from the security and inaccessibility of a movie star. A frightened girl. *I have to go, right away,* ran her thought. *Why did we ever come in here? Why did we ever talk so that she heard us?*

But this was all useless thinking. And useless talking. Myrta talked on.

"You're sure you'll be comfortable, 'bunking together,' as Freddy says? Perhaps Elizabeth could fix up the room next to Cilla's—?"

"Oh, no!" Judy said, "*please* don't bother her. We'll be perfectly comfortable." How her heart was pounding! If Elizabeth were roused now, if more tasks were heaped upon her, the way would never be cleared. Cilla would be awakened, in all probability, and Garth and Harris. Escape would be hopeless.

Myrta seemed to see nothing amiss. "All right," she said. "You girls run on, then. I think I'll read myself to sleep."

Judy had been conscious of Freddy close beside her. A worried partner. But the girl was not forgetting her self-imposed duty to guard and protect her aunt.

"You won't need any medicine tonight, will you, Aunt Myrta?" she said. "I can put the box away."

"Yes, put it away."

Freddy's face lighted as she came nearer the table at Myrta's bedside. Judy saw her almost snatch the little white box, take it across the room to a high dresser. There were two small drawers at the top. Freddy opened one, slipped the box inside and shut it. The sound seemed to echo in the room.

Out of the corner of her eye, Judy was watching Myrta. What was the expression she saw in the dark eyes? Affection, yes. Amusement? Was Myrta only pretending to cooperate with Freddy's method of nursing? Would she, later, take the medicine herself? There had been no lock on the little drawer. And the woman could not be absolutely bedridden. She could get up if she wanted to. Or could she?

Judy really did not know. But this much was certain, thus far—Freddy had coaxed her mind away from the little white box. If Garth Frazer were trying to urge a poison on Myrta, it had not as yet taken too great an effect. There was time to bring the whole clouded, beastly situation into the open.

If she, Judy, would stop standing here and get to the business before her!

Freddy was closer to the door which led to her room. Judy was nearer to the bed where Myrta Mattis was lying. The woman said suddenly, "Freddy, why don't you wear your gray woolen dress?"

It was spoken so abruptly that for a moment Judy did not sense the full import. Freddy said, haltingly, "Why—I tore it. I haven't got around to mending it."

Judy saw it all then. Freddy's clothes, which Garth had asked Elizabeth to take away. Myrta did not know about this. She did not know about any of the secret, hateful things hovering over her beautiful head.

"Not that I don't enjoy seeing you in that robe, my dear," Myrta said swiftly. "Or your lounging pajamas. But seeing Judy—"

Freddy managed a laugh. "You *are* getting better Aunt Myrta. When you start noticing clothes, it's a sure sign!"

Clothes. That was another piece in the puzzle. *Costumes.* That was another. The rack of costumes in Freddy's clothes closet. The rich, extravagant things which, Freddy had said, were not gaudy on Myrta.

All at once the truth dawned on Judy.

"Why," she said, staring at the woman's face, "*You're Lucia Grayson!*"

Freddy gave a kind of a little gasp behind her, but Judy could not turn to her then. She was keyed up with the discovery of the moment, elated. The woman in the bed said nothing, but a dark flush spread over her face, spreading from her pointed chin to her high cheek bones.

Judy said, "Aren't you? Aren't you Lucia Grayson?"

Myrta's lips moved before the words came. "I—I was," she said at last. "My real name is Mattis—Myrta Mattis."

"Lucia Grayson," Judy said, lost in bliss. "I have such a lot of your recordings. *Still As The Night,* and *Evening Star,* and *Then You'll Remember Me.* And lots more. I've seen pictures of you. But you don't, I mean, your pictures don't do you justice. You're so much more beautiful. And you're *young!*"

She had been caught up, swept away. She knew that Freddy had come to her side, and was whispering something to her. But Judy did not hear. She was looking at Myrta Mattis. The hands in the soft folds of the bed jacket came up, beseechingly—almost, it seemed, piteously.

"You—don't—understand," Myrta said slowly. "I haven't—sung for some time."

"That's because you've been ill," Judy said. "But you're getting well again. Freddy says you are, and she ought to know. And I think you look wonderful. Besides, anybody who can sing like you—well, you'll just go right on singing. You can't help it!"

Freddy was openly pulling at Judy's arm. Her blue eyes said, surely, "Don't say any more about it! Let's hurry and go!"

Judy said aloud, contritely, "I'm sorry if I tired you

—but I was so—thrilled! I—we better get to bed now." She began to edge away. "Good night."

The lovely fingers of Myrta Mattis's hands were twined together, showing white at the knuckles. Some of the flush had disappeared from the olive cheeks. Shaking her head, she denied, "You didn't tire me, Judy. Such honest praise, from you, is a rare tribute. But I," she leaned back against the pillows, "I think I'll go to sleep now."

There was another lamp, nearer to the desk. Freddy turned it out. The room was quiet, save for the wind. One of the tall windows rattled. It kept on rattling while the girls went quietly to the door that led to Freddy's room. The blond girl paused.

"Sweet dreams." She smiled. "Call me if you want me, Aunt Myrta."

"I will," the woman said. Judy was relieved to see that she appeared quite composed on the pillows. "I'll be looking forward to seeing you both in the morning. Good night."

Judy was uncomfortable with the conviction that she had made a mistake. She never should have mentioned the name of Lucia Grayson. Myrta Mattis seemed to want to forget that second self. But how could she ever expect to do that? No matter how many names she took, it was she who had made Lucia Grayson synonymous with a glorious, golden voice. That was something she could never change. And why should she want to change it?

Freddy was closing the door of her room. Neither girl had said a word. Nor did they speak until they stood, framed in the mirror over the dresser.

Judy sighed. "I'm sorry, Freddy."

"You needn't be," Freddy said quietly, thoughtfully. "In a way, I'm glad."

"Are you?" Judy's head came up quickly.

"Yes, I am. I think, maybe, it might help her. You—you don't understand about it, and I don't myself—all of it, I mean—but Aunt Myrta wouldn't let any of us mention her singing. Elizabeth told me the minute I got here. But, of course, I never thought to warn you." Freddy sighed. "How could I guess we'd go in there? Or that you'd recognize her?"

"Well," Judy said emphatically, "I think she's one of the most gifted singers of our time. And I think," her mouth was a straight line, "I think I won't lose another minute in getting out of here!"

Freddy drew her breath in sharply, but said nothing.

"You see," Judy went on, moving nearer to the bed, nearer to the white cape, "it was one thing making sure your aunt was safe. But now, it's more important than ever."

"You mean—because she—sang?"

"I mean, well, I was kind of an interested spectator before. That's not it, exactly. I was anxious about her and you, too, Freddy. Because I liked you, the moment I saw your teddy bear and that Scottie."

"In my apartment." Freddy was smiling shakily.

"Yes. At the Doyles'. Well, I liked you then. It seemed as though we'd been friends for a long time."

"I feel that way, too, Judy."

"And now your aunt," Judy went on. "I know her, too. Her voice. Why, I couldn't any more let anything happen to you, or her!" Judy broke off. "Listen, Freddy, you go over to the door. See if the way's clear. I'm going to get into my coat and hat."

Freddy leaned back against the dresser, her face the picture of misery. "It's so late, Judy. It's such a horrible night!"

"We went over all that before," Judy reminded her. "Things aren't going to get any better. They'll get worse." She had her hat on, and lifted her coat, thrusting her arms in the sleeves. "You couldn't possibly keep me out of this now. Not after being in there, with her."

Still Freddy did not move. "Maybe *I* could go," she said in a hoarse whisper. "You stay here and—"

"And have your aunt calling to you! No, this is my job. Now, hurry over to the door. I want to look in the mirror and get this cape on right."

With shoulders that bent under their heavy weight of fear, Freddy went to the door. Judy stood before the dresser, lifting the cape, tying it under her chin. She brought the collar up, over her head. Holding it in place with one hand, she rummaged with the other in a small, silver notion box. She found a safety pin and deftly fastened the collar.

If it had been another time, a different set of circumstances, it might have been funny, the bunglesome effect she saw in the mirror. Only the little lamp was lighted, the lamp on the round table. Judy's back was toward it, as she peered at her mirrored self. Bunglesome or not, it was what she wanted. A blur of white. Her coat would show, but not enough to matter. Her shoes—Judy thought of the snow, and looked up again, away from her feet.

But Freddy thought of it too. Her face was grimly serious. "You'll catch your death of cold," she whispered.

"I'll keep moving," Judy promised. "Do I look like a spirit?" For Freddy's sake, she was trying to make it as easy as possible, but the thought of the stairs, of the door under the kitchen steps, of the inner basement with its "torture room," that was not at all amusing.

Freddy nodded. "You look all right," she said. "Oh, Judy!"

"Is anybody out there?" Judy cut in. "Is everyone in bed by now, do you think?"

"I think so. I haven't heard a sound."

They both stood close to the hallway door, listening. Around the whole house, the storm was lashing. From somewhere, the living-room, perhaps, a clock chimed three times—a quarter to eleven, Judy decided. She said suddenly, "How'll I see my way down in the basement? Is there a light there?"

"No, there isn't." Freddy paused a moment. "You'll have to take the lantern. It's in the low cupboard under the kitchen sink. Matches are there, too." She seemed to choke. "Oh, Judy, be careful, won't you? Do you think you can find your way down the stairs? You can't light a light there!"

"There's a bannister," Judy remembered. "I can feel my way down." But there was something else she had to know. About the steps that led finally to the inner basement. "Under the kitchen steps," she said, "is there a door *there?* And how do I—?"

"It's a door with a kind of spring," Freddy cut in swiftly. "You push in on it, and it'll give—inward. Then you have to be careful. It's like crawling out onto the top of a ladder. The steps go right straight down."

Judy took a deep breath. "Whoever planned this house," she said, "had an imagination, all right. Or was it Indians?"

"It was Myrta's grandmother. I—I've often thought she must have been afraid of something. Or maybe had a treasure."

What they said was not important. What they both felt, and wished they might avoid, was the belief that the way was not clear.

Judy braced her shoulders. "I don't hear anything," she whispered. "And I've got it all straight. The lantern and matches under the sink. The kind of a trapdoor and the ladder steps down to the basement. From there I go out under the back steps. That right?"

"That's right," Freddy said under her breath. "I'll open the door, just a little." She did so, and then, again, they both waited. Nothing seemed alive except the storm.

Judy advised, "Keep a stiff upper lip, Freddy. I'll see you in the morning." And before the blond girl could hold her back, Judy moved swiftly past her into the hallway.

She heard Freddy's soft gasp, and the door close. She stood, getting her eyes accustomed to the dim light. It came from the stairs, from a tall window above the lower landing.

"That's where they lead into the kitchen," Judy thought. "If I can get just that far, I'll be all right."

She moved nearer to the stairs, her hand found the railing, and she started on down. One step, and another. And then she heard the soft movement far below, from somewhere on the first floor.

Fear struck at her heart, a cold, gripping terror that made her feet numb to her bidding. She stood staring down below, her heart pounding so it seemed to be throbbing in her throat, choking her.

Someone was coming up the short flight from the kitchen. She knew this, and still she stood, helpless, staring down.

A dark figure emerged. A hand reached upward, whitely, perhaps to turn on a light. Or that was what it looked like—Judy never knew. For in the next instant, the figure paused. A scream of abject terror broke over the stairs, and while the piercing echoes still rang in Judy's ears, the figure toppled, falling with a thick, dull sound.

CHAPTER SEVEN

THROUGH THE TORTURE ROOM

How she ever found the courage to move on down the steps, Judy never knew. Perhaps it was that she feared the graver danger lurking from above, in the wide hallway, where the bedroom doors would be flung open one by one as each occupant sought to discover the cause of the piercing cry. Whoever had come to that first landing, whoever had cried out—that person had been even more terrified than she. Terrified at *her*. So frightened, indeed, as to have fainted, for there was no further movement from below.

Judy realized that she was clutching at the banister, edging downward, step by step. If she could only go faster, get down the second flight, and reach the kitchen before she should be discovered!

She came to the first, the wider landing, where the painting hung. The picture in its frame was a mammoth, square blur. Judy went on, past it. Overhead, she heard the first of the opening doors. Not directly overhead, but farther down the hall. She guessed it was the door of the room which Garth and Harris jointly occupied.

"Hurry! Hurry!" she breathed the words, almost

sobbed them, and came to the square place which would presently lead down to the kitchen.

The stairs were so wide! There must be room enough to get by, down to where she could find the lantern and the secret wall opening, and traverse the last lap of her treacherous journey.

There just had to be room enough to get by, Judy told herself again, frantically, because she knew that whoever had screamed and fallen lay senseless on the stairs before her.

Little if any light reached the spot directly under the tall window. The stairs were dark, and the figure was in deep shadow. Judy's foot touched something soft before she realized she had stepped so close.

For the fraction of a second, she paused. Overhead, the alarm had grown into a booming volume of sound. Doors slammed. Voices rose to a high pitch.

Garth Frazer called out, "Who's there? What's the matter?"

"I thought I heard someone fall," Harris said, and his voice sounded foggy with sleep as though he had just awakened.

A rush of footsteps could be heard. Cilla cried, "Oh, Garth, what is it? What's happened?"

And Freddy must have come out of her room at the same time that Myrta opened her door, for Cilla said, "Do you know what that was, Freddy? Oh, mother, please go back to bed!"

That was not all. Freddy was saying she could not

guess what it was, and Myrta was declaring she had every intention of knowing what was going on in her own house. But Judy did not wait to hear all this.

The kitchen was black. The shades must have been pulled down, for there was no dim glow of the outside snow to guide her. Judy had knelt, hoping to explore the steps with her hands, to crawl down on all fours if she had to.

But the quiet, motionless figure was there, directly across the opening which would lead down. Judy heard a low groan, which told of growing consciousness. It would be too great a risk to try and surmount this obstacle. She might stumble or fall. That would cut off her escape.

Nor was there any turning back to go on up the stairs. But, to the left, a branching flight went undoubtedly to the living-room. Judy could just barely see the rim of the steps. Windows along the front of the house, where there were no drawn blinds or tightly pulled drapes, let in a murky grayness which was enough light to see in hazily.

Crouching low, Judy slowly made her way downward. It was then, when she had reached the lower floor, that she heard Myrta saying this was her own house, and she would do as she pleased in it.

Despite her perilous situation, Judy thought fleetingly that the sick woman showed evidence of still remaining strength. She must have come to the door of her room by herself, and she must still be standing up there in the hall.

It was *for her,* Judy thought, and *for Freddy,* for rightness and certainty against the strange and unreal power that Garth Frazer was exerting over the Mattis house, that Myrta was struggling so bravely.

Judy told herself that she could not fail, that she must find a path through this tumult and confusion. She must get to Grace, somehow, anyhow!

She remembered Grace Doyle with pleasant recollection—the white apron over her business dress. And Marion turning out the lights in Freddy's room. The two of them, waiting so patiently for the girl to come back.

"She'll come back!" Judy thought grimly, as slowly, stealthily, she tiptoed across a room whose dark ceiling was lost in obscurity overhead. Her hand touched something smooth and cold, standing upright—the face of a clock! A clock which was still, not ticking. Her feet sank into a patch of thicker carpet, a small throw rug over the general carpeting. Once she stumbled and would have fallen, but her hand held out before her hit against the back of a low, overstuffed couch.

The voices were growing nearer. Footsteps were coming down the stairs.

Garth said, "You others wait here. I'll go down and see who it is."

"Why don't you turn on the light?" Cilla cried, her voice taut, shrill.

"It's out of order, up here," Garth said. "But it works from the landing. I'll light it there."

The footsteps sounded heavier. Harris said gruffly, "I'll come with you."

Such a small thing for Judy to be grateful for! A two-way switch which was out of order, which did not work from the top of the stairs. The delay in Garth's going downstairs in the semi-darkness gave Judy another precious gain in time. She had glimpsed a high, wide archway which must be divided at the top. It seemed that a horizontal opening ran the full width of it, as though a shelf were built in overhead. This, she found, was true, for there came, faintly in the gloom, the gleam of silver, of glass. Judy made her way to the archway, but suddenly stopped, her fear chilling her to the marrow again as she saw a white figure looming before her.

There was no sound, no movement, until Judy raised one hand blindly, as though to ward off the apparition. She saw the identical movement repeated by the mysterious figure and realized the truth—she stood before a mirror.

In that instant, the light went on over the stairs.

Harris cried, "Why, it's Elizabeth!"

Cilla's voice came again, shrill with surprise, "Elizabeth!"

Garth said, "It's all right. She's coming to."

Three of the household had spoken, Garth, Harris, and Cilla. Not Myrta. And not Freddy. Had the blond

The Apparition Repeated the Movement

girl succeeded in putting Myrta back to bed again? Even while Judy edged away from the shaft of light which came from the stairs, down into the living-room behind her, she hoped that Freddy had quieted her aunt.

So it was Elizabeth who had screamed, and fainted. Elizabeth who had seen her on the stairs.

Judy rushed frantically into the next room, the dining-room. Its walls and ceiling were equally vast, away from the glow on the stairs, yet Judy caught the gleam of a mirror at the back of a built-in buffet the full width of the room. Heavy, carved silver was set upon it, big pieces of tableware.

And *now* where should she go, the girl asked herself. Into the kitchen, of course. She must get to the kitchen, to the cupboard underneath the sink first of all—for the lantern. Without that, she could never hope to find her way through the difficult intricacies of the inner basement.

But that was the way Freddy had outlined her way of escape when neither of them had anticipated the commotion on the stairs. Only—poor old Elizabeth was lying there, the center of a general hubbub. Could the same plan be worked out now? Garth and Harris must be near the top of the short flight that led up from the kitchen. Perhaps Judy would get only that far when they would come down, discover her. It would be far worse than if Garth had found her in Freddy's room. What explanation could she possibly give of the white cape, of her stealthy leavetaking?

But what about Freddy? Maybe Freddy would think of something. She knew of Judy's plight. The thing to do, then, was to wait, and listen.

Judy had come to a door which she was certain would lead into the kitchen. It was a swinging door, and noiselessly she pushed it slightly inward. She stood, every nerve tense, and found that it was Myrta or good fortune that came to her assistance.

Myrta was saying, "Help her up here, to my room."

Garth said, as though he were repeating his question, "*But what did you see, Elizabeth?* Tell us!"

"Please, Garth," Myrta said. "Let her get her breath."

And then Judy heard Freddy: "It's all right, Elizabeth. There was nothing there. Don't you worry."

"*Nothing there!*" Cilla snapped. "The way the woman shrieked, you'd think it was *seven ghosts!*"

More murmurs, words cropping out above, made a hum of sound, but the whole was drowned as Elizabeth was assisted up the stairs.

To Myrta's room, Judy thought. For a while Myrta would be busy with the old woman. Or Freddy would be taking care of her. It would probably be such a shock to Myrta that she would be unequal to the strain. It would be far better for Judy, if this were the case. If Myrta were only too weak to notice her absence—because, sooner or later, she would be bound to question Freddy. Where was Judy? Hadn't Judy heard the disturbance?

But that was only a possibility in the future. Now Judy had reached the tile that outlined and was part of the sink. Her fingers moved down over the cupboard beneath it, found a knob. She knelt and opened a small door. Groping inward, her hands found only cooking utensils. Something sharp—a vegetable grater. It clicked against a kettle and the sound seemed mountainous. Judy paused to listen. The drone of voices continued overhead and the girl discovered the second knob, which meant the other, matching door.

Almost at once, she knew she had located the matches. A paper carton, open and half used. She took out one of the boxes, reached in and brought out a fistful of the sticks. These she crammed into the pocket of her coat.

Farther back, near something which might be a food chopper, was the lantern. Judy turned it sidewise, brought it out carefully.

She had what she needed now, the lantern and the matches—and no one was coming down the stairs.

They were all up there, she thought. All save Martin. Freddy thought he had gone to the garage rooms. Perhaps he had. Freddy had believed that Elizabeth had gone, too. But the old woman had still been in the house. Busy, perhaps, with some last-minute task due to the late arrivals. Everyone, then, except Martin, was at this moment accounted for.

Of this, Judy made sure, because she knew it would be impossible to find her way to the trap-door under the stairs, to the steps there which led down, as Freddy had said, like a ladder. Freddy knew the way. Freddy could find it. But Judy feared she might make a misstep. Stumble, and fall down that invisible ladder.

No. She had to risk lighting just one match.

But first, though it used up another precious moment, Judy paused again to listen. She could hear the murmur of voices from upstairs, and guessed the speakers must have gathered in one of the rooms, Myrta's perhaps—because Myrta had said to bring Elizabeth into her room.

On the floor, kneeling, close to the sink, Judy heard a door open and the voices rose.

Cilla's came first, with little sympathy: "It's too bad you had to wake us up, scare us half to death!"

Then Harris: "Now, Cilla, take it easy. You might be old some day."

They were coming out into the hallway.

Garth said, "I'll have a look around. Want to come with me, Harris?"

"Yes. Wait till I get into my clothes."

Cilla snapped, "She should be out in the garage, where she belongs."

Judy wanted to light the match, to creep over to the invisible door under the steps, but she was held back by the wish to learn more, if possible, of the manner in which Myrta and Freddy were reacting to Elizabeth's fright. And there was extra time now. Harris was coming down with Garth to look over the house, but first he was going to dress. There was time, not much, but a little. Judy did not add, even to herself, the real reason why she was waiting here, crouching in the dark. It was because she was afraid of what was to come, afraid of descending, alone, into the inner basement, to the "torture room."

Freddy must have come out into the hall. Judy heard her say, "Aunt Myrta says it will be all right for Elizabeth to sleep on the porch. If the door's left open, she'll be warm enough. I'll fix up the cot for her."

"The perfect little housekeeper!" Cilla sneered. "Isn't it too bad you haven't a home of your own to manage?"

"I have," Freddy said quietly. "I think it's bad taste to quarrel at a time like this, Cilla. We'll only worry Aunt Myrta. She's had enough excitement for one night. Elizabeth, too."

"Oh," Cilla fumed, "you make me sick!"

Judy heard her walking overhead, as though she were stamping in high heels. Then came the slamming of a door.

Freddy must have moved, too, toward Myrta's room. "I'll have the cot ready in a little while, Elizabeth. And then, Aunt Myrta, I'll be ready to tuck you in."

Myrta said something, but Judy knew that she could not wait another moment. Harris was getting ready to come down with Garth. She had to start on her dark journey at once.

The match, which she struck on the linoleum, flamed high. The light danced in a high peak. Judy held it forward, and saw the space under the short flight of steps where the hidden door must be. She blew out the light, laid the half-burned stick on the sink, and crept across the floor. She was conscious of the people overhead, but could never have repeated what they were saying. Her mind was ahead now, on the ladder-like steps, the hidden door which led to them.

She came to touch solid wood, the floor board. Her fingers moved upward. And again, she paused.

She must have a light again. Not a match, that was not enough. She could light the lantern. It would take only a moment to open the hidden door, and then she would be sure. The lantern's light would hold.

But, first, another match. Then to light the wick. That took more time than she thought. The thing had to be lifted up, the slide, was it called? Lanterns were not among the things Judy was used to.

Upstairs, Harris was saying, "I'm all set. Let's go and find Elizabeth's ghost."

Judy's fingers fumbled. The flame that dashed over the wick was too high. She must turn it down.

Hurry, she told herself frantically, *Oh, hurry!* Why

had she waited? Maybe now it was too late. Maybe the men would come down and find her. After all her talk about going ahead and getting help as soon as possible, what had she done? She had hesitated because she was afraid. Now, Judy admitted it to herself. At the side of the steps she was afraid to push in against the wood, which before seemed a solid enough panel. What if the door had been nailed shut? What if she could not open it? Freddy told her about a time long ago. Things might have changed since then.

But they had not changed. The door was there. Judy's fingers were pressing inward, moving with the door. The lantern was on the floor beside her. Its light showed the steps, or the top step. So, even when you were afraid, you somehow managed to go on, doing what you had to do. Even when you admitted to yourself that you were sick with terror, your numbed hands obeyed you, your leaden feet did your bidding.

Garth and Harris were coming down the wide stairs over Judy's head. But she was inside the low, dark opening. Despite the cumbersome coat with the cape over it, despite the awkwardly swinging lantern, she was inside. She was gripping the top of the ladder steps, swinging herself downward, feeling the lower steps beneath her feet.

But the door above her had remained open. Judy had to give it a push from the inside to close it.

Had Garth and Harris heard the sound? For there

had been a sound, a muffled thud.

Motionless, on the narrow steps, Judy waited.

No, they had not heard the sound. They had not come in the direction of the kitchen. They had gone down the other way, where the stairway led into the living-room.

From the depths of her being, Judy drew a great sigh and continued on her way.

How many steps there were, she did not know. She was conscious only of going down, down into a black emptiness. For the lantern was in her hand, lighting up the top of the space. Cold air came to her nostrils, and the smell of moist earth. Below was the cellar, surely.

Suddenly her feet touched firm ground.

Judy held the lantern up slightly, and looked about. The place looked something like a storeroom, save that it held no provisions. There were shelves along two of the walls; the two which were narrower, for the room was rectangular in shape, perhaps twelve by six feet. An ancient, iron stove was in one corner. In another, several wooden stools were stacked one on top of the other. They would be of no use now. Nothing in here was of any use.

But, long ago, this must have been a place of refuge —a hiding place. Only little children, playing a pretend game, would call it a "torture room." Only a girl like Cilla, for instance, wanting to frighten Freddy. There was nothing here to fear. Nothing at all.

Then why was she shaking, trembling in every nerve?

"I mustn't get the jitters now," Judy said, aloud—and, low as she had spoken, the words seemed to rise thickly. She repeated, valiantly, "I'm half way. I'm safe. As far as *they're* concerned," she added. "They'll never guess where I am. How could they ever guess?"

What should she do next? She must go on, through the passage which would lead her out at the back of the house, out under the back stairs.

But where was the door?

Judy's heart began to pound again. Suppose she were trapped down in this dismal place, because it *was* a dismal place; the air, after any length of time, would choke her!

She would have no choice but to return, up the ladder steps, to the kitchen, to the house. Admit failure. Perhaps run into the two men, Garth Frazer and Harris Morley. She would be a kind of prisoner, then, along with Freddy. Garth would never let her go.

But that was foolishness. Surely there was a way out. Freddy had said so. Freddy had told her about the hidden trap door, about the ladder-like steps. She had found them exactly as the blond girl had described them. So there must be a door.

The thing to do was to turn the lantern up higher. No need to worry about the flame now. No one could be watching her. There were no windows in the "torture room."

The flame went higher in the glass bowl, and Judy lifted it, peering slowly, intently at the walls.

There was the door, of course, back of the iron stove. All she had to do was to move that stove.

She put down the lantern. Purposefully, her hands gripped the metal, reddish and rough. Judy tried to move it. It did not give an inch. The size of the thing was deceptive. It was terrifically heavy.

"I've got to get it out of the way!" she told herself frantically. "Perhaps, if I put on my gloves—?"

They were in the purse compartment of her muff. And her muff?

It was back in Freddy's room. She had forgotten it.

For a moment, that was another worry. The muff might be discovered. But if it were, Judy told herself swiftly, it would be Freddy who would find it. Maybe Freddy had found it already. And she would see that it remained out of sight.

Just one thing mattered right now—getting this stove out of the way.

With renewed purpose, Judy set to work once more. The stove could not be lifted, but it could be edged away—a painfully slow process, but putting pressure first to the left, then to the right, it could be done. It *had* to be done.

And Judy did it. She saw the space back of the stove widening until there would be room enough for her to pass through, room enough to open the door. Her hands were bruised from the unaccustomed work. Her back was aching with the strain. But the girl scarcely noticed her discomfort. She was too much occupied with the hope that ahead lay the passage which would lead her out into the open air. It might be cold, bitterly cold, outside. The snow might by now be so deep that she would have to struggle through drifts to get to the highway.

But it would be the open air. It would be free from mysterious, dark imaginings.

A lock of hair had spilled down from under the collar of Judy's cape. She pushed the curl back, tucking it swiftly under the hat band which went around at the back of her head. She thought with dismay that she might have accomplished her task faster if she had taken time to remove her coat and the white cape. But it was too cold in there to discard it—and she had to hurry, hurry.

What did it matter now, anyway? The door was there, and she could go on.

But the white cape had suffered from the ordeal, even as her hands had suffered. Dark stains streaked across it where she leaned against the stove, and where her soiled hands had touched the soft material.

"It's still mostly white," Judy told herself. "White enough so that I can get away from the house without Martin seeing me."

She tried to decide what time it was. Midnight? It must be close to twelve o'clock, certainly. In all probability, Martin had gone to bed, and to sleep. Elizabeth was anything but young, and Martin—Judy paused there in her thoughts. Elizabeth, she reminded herself, had been very much awake not so long ago. Elizabeth had been on the wide stairway, had screamed with terror at the sight of her.

Well, Judy squared her shoulders, grasped the handle of the lantern firmly. Whether Martin were awake or asleep, she was going to escape to the highway. She was going to get back to the Doyles. To tell Grace. To be again in the comfortable house with the red-splashed cloth on the kitchen table. She remembered wistfully Marion's delicious supper—it seemed to have happened in another world, in another age. But it had been this very same evening! And soon, soon, she would be back there again. And everything would be—as it should be.

The door had a wooden knob, more like a peg. Judy had to tug at it to get it open. Her hand hurt with the effort, but that was unimportant. Now she could go on down the passage.

The passage stretched before her, straight, level, as far as the lantern's rays could penetrate. For an instant, after the door closed behind her, Judy looked down that low, narrow way—and then she was moving forward.

What had Freddy said? Would there be more steps? Or would the passage lead slowly upward? Judy tried to remember, but could not. Whichever way it led, that was the way she had to go.

The light of the lantern struck against a solid wall because the passage led sharply to the left. And it did go upward, in a gentle but constant incline. The ceiling was lower. Judy had to bend her head as she went forward.

At last, she came to a door. The door was made of boards going up and down, and two heavier boards crossing against it. There was a wooden slot, where a wooden bar fitted in. Judy lifted it, pushed it back. She had to pull against this to open the door, for there was no knob. With what seemed a tremendously loud creaking, the way of escape opened before her.

Snow slashed at her in a zestful, icy gust. It hissed at the lantern's hot glass, which Judy quickly put down. She did not need it any more. She was no longer a prisoner—she was out in the open.

Bending, she put out the light and set the lantern on the earthen floor. With one step she was clear of the passage, and in relief she shut the door behind her.

The snow immediately in front of her was not so deep. The wind had whirled it into a small, gently cleared space. Ankle deep it was, and Judy walked through it for perhaps ten paces. Then she came up against a drift that seemed to bar her way.

She paused, questioning which way to turn, and heard the sound, a voice, broken, husky. The words sounded like: "It's true! I said it!" But in the sudden shock of terror, Judy was not listening, she was not prepared to listen, believing she must be alone. She turned, her eyes darted to the right, from whence the voice had come, and she saw the dark shadow of a man, his arms outspread. There was enough light to see his face, because he was coming nearer, and Judy was powerless to move. The eyes seemed to bulge whitely, with small dark beads glaring. A wide mouth was open, showing teeth in which might be a smile of triumph. The man was saying something, over and over—and coming nearer.

Judy felt herself lost in the power of that piercing gaze. Her shoulders, her body swayed beyond her control.

When she fell, she was not conscious of the cold snow against her face.

CHAPTER EIGHT

THE SPIRIT OF THE LAKE

Judy heard a choking sound coming nearer. Someone was coughing. She herself was coughing. Because she was huddled in an uncomfortable position, she was too warm. She lifted her head with a great effort. Her head was against something hard, the back of a chair. She was sitting in a chair. This seemed impossible. She tried to open her eyes. The lids seemed weighted. Her hands, too, were heavy, heavy, resting in her lap. And then she heard a voice, a woman's voice saying, "She's waking."

Rebelliously, Judy pushed her mind through the mists that shrouded her. "What has happened to me?" she thought wildly. "I have to find out—find out where I am!"

She opened her eyes, looked straight ahead. Not five feet away, a man was sitting in a straight-backed chair. He was looking at her through half-shut eyes, but not sleepily. It was as though he were trying to tear her mind apart, to search out her terrified thoughts. A light must be near him, a yellowish light, for his square face was of a yellowish color. Judy looked as long as she could into that penetrating gaze, and she thought, "It's a dream! I'll wake up in a minute. Oh, *but I am awake!*"

Her head went farther back, weakly. She saw over the man's head a tan wall with brown flowers, a picture in a round, gilded frame. It was a tinted picture, the photograph of a woman, taken long ago. The woman wore a high-necked collar. Her shoulders were black and they bulged. Her eyes looked steadily ahead, into space.

"I am awake!" Judy thought again, and drew a gasping breath. "But how did I get here?"

She remembered, then, how she had fallen in the snow. She was coming out of the "torture room." No, it was after that. She had gone through the "torture room," through the long passage. She had left the lantern, come out into the open air back of the Mattis house. She had believed the way to be clear, but it had not been clear. A man had appeared, a man with bulging eyes.

That man was before her now, standing at the left of the square-jawed one seated before her. Who were they? Why was she here? How soon would they tell her what it was all about?

Judy's lips moved as she tried to ask—to say the words, but no words came. A woman near her said, "Give her time. It takes time."

"Yes. From the place where she came, from the place of the so-called dead. It takes time." This was a man's voice, in a kind of singsong minor key.

Judy thought wildly, "The place of the so-called

dead!" and turned her head to the left, in the direction from which the man's voice had come. She saw him, tall and haggardly thin, with thick, black hair bristling over a face seamed with wrinkles. No, *gashes* would be more like it. Across the forehead, over deep-set eyes and at the sides of a drawn-out, drooping mouth. The woman who had spoken was not far from him. She was dark-haired, too, but her hair was tight against her white face. She was staring upward with a kind of fierce intensity.

The place of the so-called dead! The words rang like a knell in Judy's mind. Were these strangers the dead? No, they were very much alive. And she, Judy, was very much alive too. She felt the pain in her head, a blinding pain that drew down over her eyes. Her hand hurt, where she had cut it in her struggle to move the iron stove.

"It's a mistake," Judy tried to reassure herself. "I've come here, somehow, by a mistake," but even as the thought came, she knew how futile it was. "I was taken here, carried here," she told herself, and made herself acknowledge the truth. "I fainted, and these people brought me here. Or that man did. The one with the bulging eyes."

But *where* was she? Why were these men, this woman, staring at her so intently? What did the black-haired man mean by the "place of the so-called dead?"

"I won't talk," Judy decided, and closed her eyes

"Why Do They Stare at Me?" Judy Wondered

again, trying to arrive at some reasonable explanation. But she could not close her eyes to what she had already seen of the room where she was. It was low-ceilinged, with walls of dull tan and brown. The furniture was a queer mixture of almost antique vintage and some wicker. There was a china cabinet in one corner. It had a red vase perched on top. This Judy had seen, but it was of no help to her memory. She had never been here before, and she could not even imagine where she was.

She thought, "I'll keep my eyes closed, and listen. They don't act as though they'll harm me in any way. I guess I'm safe enough. I'll wait."

"Fainted again," said the man, the one Judy knew had the shock of black hair.

"Yes," said the woman. "Give her more time."

Judy could scarcely control the quivering of her lips. She wanted to cry out, "Who are you? Why don't you tell me why I am here?"

She heard the voice of the man with the bulging eyes—the man who had appeared when she had believed she was free.

"It's the truth!" he said huskily. "I believed with Hugen. He said it and I said it!"

Then Judy became aware of more persons present than she had yet seen. At her right, there was a low archway. Judy could not see where it led, into some adjoining room where others must be grouped about, waiting in this strange, unreal manner for her to "waken."

Judy still could not see these others, but she heard them talking in a dull, dissenting murmur.

The man with the bulging eyes said, "You don't believe it?" and the low voices stopped.

"I never said I didn't believe it." This was another woman. "Would I be here if I was going to doubt?"

Judy found herself unable to keep up the pretense any longer. Despite her growing panic, she let her head turn slowly to the right, and through half-shut eyes she looked in the direction of the archway, from whence the last voice had come.

The woman was of medium height, light brown hair pulled back of her ears and falling in uneven lengths to her shoulders. Her cheeks were sunken and too heavily rouged. In the slantwise beams of the yellow lamp, the rouge accentuated the hollowness of her face, giving her a witch-like look. With the woman were two men. One was a slight, middle-aged figure, with a light, dispirited cap pulled over his face. The other was an immensely tall man, who stood with his arms crossed over his chest. His hair was gray and unruly. Down one cheek, a scar cut to the corner of puffy, rebellious lips.

The girl closed her eyes again, and kept them closed. She felt suddenly very weary. Horribly tired. So much had happened—too much, crammed in too short a time.

Almost, as if it were not very important, Judy wondered again about the time. What time was it? Midnight? No, it must be later than that. But it was still dark, very dark.

Time. That was what some of these people were talking about. Only they wanted to give *her* time to wake up. They all seemed to want her to wake up.

Why? Judy did not recognize a single voice or face. An ill-assorted group of persons, none of them well dressed. Five men and two women. Who were they? And above all, what interest had they in Judy Garland?

The dizziness passed as swiftly as it had come. But Judy felt the need of air, more air, or she would choke. One of her hands came up to open her coat at the throat. She found that it was unbuttoned. She thought of the cape she had tied about her neck, the collar over her head. The cape was gone. Something moved against her other hand. Her little fur hat—it was on her lap. Judy's fingers dug into it. She held on as though it were a treasure about to be snatched away. And, from some unnamable source, she drew the strength to sit up straighter, to open her eyes, because it seemed that she had awaked at last from a distorted dream. That she was again herself.

The woman at her left, the one with the uplifted face, said, "Ah! That's better!"

The man with the shock of hair said, "The journey is completed. She has done well. Many do not survive."

Judy thought to herself, "*I'm* going to survive. And I'm going to make them tell me where I am, and the meaning of this!"

Looking directly ahead, she faced the half-open boring eyes of the man in the chair. For a moment, the small spark of resolution died out. But Judy summoned her courage. She met his eyes squarely.

"Why am I here?" she asked him.

The man only nodded. He turned to the fellow with the bulging eyes, and this one rubbed his hands together. It was as though a careful experiment in which they had been engaged, and which had resulted in countless failures, had suddenly succeeded beyond their dreams.

All the others, the three in the farther room, beyond the arch, and the man and woman grouped at Judy's left, they, too, seemed a part of a tremendously important hush, a moment of expectation rewarded.

And Judy knew anger, sharp and swift. They had brought her here, or they had a part in bringing her here—against her will. What right had they? How dared they? To her simple questions, a blank wall of faces—no, of smirking faces—was her only answer.

"I want to know why you have brought me here," Judy demanded more loudly, her eyes going about the room. She saw that the three had come closer to each other under the low archway.

They exchanged looks, these and the others at the girl's left, as though a kind of an explanation were due from them, but uncertain who should give it. Their glances settled finally upon the man with the piercing eyes.

He shook his head in what passed for a kind of pity. "You must not overtax your strength," he said. His voice had a metallic ring. "You have suffered, you must understand."

"I certainly have," Judy admitted. "But I don't intend to go on suffering. I mean to be free. You let me go—!"

"No!" the woman at her left almost sobbed. "Oh, no! Be still, please be still!" She appealed to the man with the half-shut eyes. "Is it always like that, Hugen? *You* know. You saw it before. No one of us ever did." The woman clasped her hands. "Oh, I wish I hadn't come!" she cried.

"Quiet!" said the man at her side. "There's no turning back now. This is what you were asking. Now you know."

The man called Hugen said, "It is this way, usually. They come unwillingly. And, as Martin told you, take form from the lake itself."

The group drew in closer, talking softly, earnestly. But Judy did not hear what they were saying. She did not try to hear.

"As Martin told you!" Hugen had said. *Martin.* Martin was Elizabeth's husband. Martin was the guardian of the Mattis house. Martin had followed her to the back door, had almost caught her.

Was it Martin who had actually caught her as she fell into the snow, after leaving the dark underground passage? She had never seen whoever it was. Hugen seemed to mean the man with the bulging eyes. That must be Martin.

And what else had this Hugen said? About "taking form from the lake itself?"

Judy heard her own voice, "Did you think I came from the lake?"

The room was almost shaken, as though a thunderclap had sounded, no, something much bigger: an earthquake. Seven pairs of eyes were riveted upon her, staring at her.

The man with the bulging eyes, the man Judy knew must be Martin, raised his arms high over his head. He seemed to implore an invisible power. "It's true!" he said again huskily. "I said it, Hugen. After all these years. I believed it!"

He turned to Hugen. "Now they know," he said. "They know that what you told us was the truth. You saw it before." He faced the group in the archway. "You won't complain about the storm now, will you? No! You'll believe what your eyes tell you!"

The thin, hollow-cheeked woman quavered, "I never said I didn't believe. I paid my share, didn't I? I came out here—waited all this time."

The big man with the scarred face said, "We waited long enough. When do we begin?"

"Yes," said the fellow with the cap, "we got to think

about getting back again."

Judy made herself stand. "I don't know what you're talking about," she said, and was surprised that her voice sounded so firm, "and I don't specially care to know. I have to get back to the city. And I have to hurry."

"To the city!" the dark woman wailed. "Oh, no! Oh, you poor thing!"

Even while she hotly resented being called a "poor thing," Judy knew it sounded funny. But perhaps that was what she was to them, a *poor thing*. Her appearance was certainly dreadful, with her scratched hands. Her face must be a sight, too.

The woman's solicitude sounded funny because it was evident that none of these people knew who she was.

They thought she was a spirit—that she had come from the lake! Judy felt herself growing stronger, taller. She could think now, clearly. And she could fight back. There would be no more of this woeful staring at her.

But the man Hugen was not staring at her reverently, or with anything like sympathy. The gleam in his eye was cold, calculating. He looked like a wary hunter, as though the animal he thought he had trapped had suddenly escaped, and was ready to spring at him.

In a blinding flash of understanding, Judy put enough of the crazily scattered pieces together to form a whole.

Martin said that now the others knew that *what Hugen had told them was the truth*. Hugen had "seen it before." Martin had never seen, but he had believed. And the woman in the archway had "paid her share."

It was a kind of swindle. A spirit swindle!

Hugen had misled this group of poor, deluded people, had probably made them pay heavily to see his "spirit of the lake."

But how had he known that Judy would be on hand this night precisely? How had he known when to assemble his group? It could not have been easy, not on a night like this, to get people together, especially for a performance of doubtful outcome.

Hugen, watching her narrowly, was saying, "You will get back. All in good time. You have nothing to fear."

Judy said, "Thank you." He was talking to her directly, telling her to behave herself, to comply by being an obedient "spirit."

But the girl had no intention of obliging him.

She was in the garage. Luckily, she had guessed that much. These rooms were the home of Martin and Elizabeth. Elizabeth would not be coming here tonight. She was probably asleep now, on the cot which Freddy had prepared on the porch. The whole Mattis household was, undoubtedly, asleep. Perhaps Freddy was still awake. The blond girl would be wondering about Judy's lonely journey in the storm, wondering if she had managed to return to the Doyles safely.

Time had been lost, but not so much time. The garage was near the house. Martin had met Judy as she had come from the inner basement. He must have brought her here at once. Then she had wakened. No, not so much time had been lost.

And no more would be lost. Judy had every intention of breaking away. She turned suddenly to Martin. "How did you know I would come here tonight?" she said.

The man's eyes seemed to pop from his head. "I saw you," he said. "I saw you coming up from the lake. Through the trees."

"From the lake?" Judy said. "It's frozen, isn't it?"

Martin shook his head. "That don't matter," he said. "I saw you. I knew! Then you disappeared."

"Then I went in the house," Judy explained. "And when I came out—"

Hugen's voice rang out: "She has not cut free the bonds as yet. I think we will need a time of peace, of rest."

The man with the heavy black hair said, "Yes. You're right." He crossed over to the archway. The dark woman went with him. "Come," he said to the others. "We'll wait out here."

Hugen was sending them away. That meant that Judy would be alone with those eyes which were biting savagely. The man had risen. He was almost six feet tall. He held his hands before him, rubbing the palms together.

Judy was suddenly horribly afraid—afraid to be left alone at the mercy of Hugen, who could not possibly be in his right mind. Or if he were, if he were mercilessly preying upon the superstition of these persons, taking their money under false pretenses, he was perhaps even more to be feared.

The girl took a step after the retreating Martin, the last to leave.

"Martin," she said, taking his arm. "Wait."

"No," he replied, and she could feel the tremor that ran through him. "No. You obey Hugen. He knows. We others—we have to wait."

How the wretch had fooled them, Judy thought. What fools they were! How blind! How could they believe she had come from the lake, from frozen Lake Oleen. A spirit! Something from another world, that must regain life. Something from a place of "so-called death."

But they did believe Hugen.

And now Judy was left alone with the man. He went over to where she stood in the archway. His hand was on her arm, not gently. "Sit down," he said, motioning to the chair from which the girl had risen.

For a moment, the girl glared her defiance, but only for a moment. She knew that she had made a mistake in letting Hugen see that she understood his hold over these people. She should have pretended to comply with his wishes.

But what were his wishes? To have her act the part of a spirit? It was a daring enterprise to trap a girl, kidnap her, carry her off and expect to have a ready-made medium on a moment's notice.

Judy seated herself.

"That's better," Hugen said.

Judy smiled. Did he guess the effort it took? "I try to be agreeable," she said. "Now, I wonder if you'd tell me something. How did you know I would be here this evening?"

The man seated himself beside her. "Martin told you. He saw you."

"I don't mean that," Judy said. "I mean, the second time. When I came out of the house."

"He saw you then, too. He was waiting for you."

"And he thought I came up out of the lake?"

"That's what he says. Martin is—deeply impressionable."

It had been, outwardly, a polite conversation, but sharp, invisible little knives pricked every word. Judy made no effort to hide the blade of her scorn when she repeated, "Deeply impressionable. So are all those other poor fools you brought out here tonight!"

The man smiled, a twitching of one end of his mouth, and took out a pack of cigarettes. "Martin brought them out," he corrected her. He chose a cigarette, lighted it. "He also called me. I was very much surprised to know that he had seen the Spirit."

"I can imagine it," Judy said hotly. "You told them there was such a thing, you got them to believe it, but when Martin said he saw it, you must have been rather upset."

"Oh, I was," he agreed coolly. "If you hadn't come along at the right moment, I would have had a great deal of unpleasant explaining to do. Or else," he smiled crookedly again, "I could have simply blamed Martin."

"And sent them all back home," Judy put in. "Promising a better spirit act next time."

"That's about the size of it," Hugen agreed. He drew deeply at the cigarette, exhaled, crushed it out on an ashtray. His face underwent a change. There was no mask over it now. "But you did happen along," he said, bending nearer. Judy drew back at the baleful glare in the boring eyes. "You did happen along," he repeated. "And if you want to leave here, Miss Garland, you'll do exactly as you're told."

Miss Garland!

"Oh, yes, I know you," he said smoothly. "In spite of the fact that you must have had a difficult time making your exit from the Mattis place."

"A difficult time—?" Judy breathed.

The man motioned to her face. "Or was it a cat in a coalbin?"

Judy's hands went to her cheeks. "It's no affair of yours," she flared, "how I look!"

"Right now, it is. None of the rest suspects who

you are. At least, I'm almost sure they don't. They were looking for a *spirit,* you see. While I—well, I was expecting no one in particular."

"You mean, then, that I'll do?" Judy asked.

"You'll have to."

The girl came to her feet. "I'm sorry, Mr. Hugen, but I think you'll have to find another spirit. I have to get to the city—in a hurry."

Hugen was standing, coming to his feet soundlessly, like an animal.

"Oh, no, you're not in that great a hurry, not until we finish the business at hand. They'll be getting impatient out there in Martin's kitchen. They want their money's worth. And you'll give it to them!"

Judy felt waves of terror mounting in her throat. She fought them down, but could not keep her eyes from darting about the room. There must be a door, a way out. She had not remembered coming in, she had been unconscious then. But there had to be a door. The thought whirled through her head, taking on a kind of a hateful melody, the fragment of a song she wanted to forget. Looking for a door! Where was the door? There had to be a door! How often had she thought the words, spoken them, in the past hours?

The yellow light seemed to rise to the ceiling. It came from a lamp, a tall lamp—at her left, where the man with the shock of hair had been. And the woman with the reverent look. The yellow light twisted and writhed and Judy thought, "I must not faint. I dare

"No, You're Not in a Hurry," Hugen Told Her

not faint."

Not far from the lamp was the door. It looked dark and old. There was a large key in the lock.

Her hand was up, over her forehead, when her eyes found it. Perhaps Hugen had not noticed. Judy looked away, kept her hands up over her face. She said weakly, "I'm so upset. This is so strange. I—I don't know what to do."

Hugen seemed satisfied. "Do as I tell you," he said flatly. "You haven't any choice."

Judy mentally agreed: "That's what I have to do. Pretend I'll do as he says. And get to that door the first chance!" But she did not speak.

She looked at him, not letting herself be bewildered again by those piercing eyes. She saw him for what he was, a trickster, preying on the faith of humble people. They might believe him to be a master mind, in tune with some of the higher forces of nature. But he was, after all, only a man, and not much of a man! If Judy were to pass him on the street, he would never have claimed her attention. He was not a commanding figure, not by any means. His gray suit was cut in a fashion well outmoded, pinched in at the waist. His shoes were cracked. They bulged out slightly over the soles. Keeping her hand over her eyes, making him believe she was weakly complying with his wishes, she murmured softly, "I—I don't know."

"Oh, yes, you do know!" The man was gloating, overjoyed. "You don't want to go back to the house again, do you?" This was a direct hit, this was thrusting his success into her face.

"Back to the house?" Judy repeated, puzzled.

Hugen nodded. A wise smile distorted his mouth. "I'd say you weren't exactly welcome in the Mattis house. Judging from," his eyes went from her scratched cheeks to her wet shoes, "general appearances." He shook his head. "No, you don't want to go back." His voice lowered, became almost confidential, "Let's understand each other. For some reason or other, you're in a jam of some kind out here. I don't know anything about that, and I'm not asking any questions. That's *your* business. Now, I'm in a jam, too. And that's *my* business. But if you want to get away from here, you'll go through this act for us. Get me?"

Judy, watching his face as though hypnotized, could only nod slowly. Hugen meant it. *If she wanted to get away from here!* He did not add *alive,* but that was what he meant, she was sure.

"I'd better make him think I'll go through with it!" Judy resolved. "Perhaps, I'll have to, actually. Perhaps—?" Her mind seemed to strike a hidden spark then, a brightly shining spark. There *was* a way out. It was not easy. But she might be able to accomplish it. No, she *had* to do it. But now she must give in—completely.

"What shall I do?" she asked quietly. "You'll have to tell me."

"Now, you're talking," the man said, and would have patted her on the shoulder, only Judy drew away quickly.

"They're talking out there," she said quickly, to cover her distasteful motion. "We'll have to hurry."

"You're right about that," Hugen said. "It's a terrible night. They'll have to walk across the lake."

"Across the lake?" Judy repeated, not believing her ears.

"Sure. The roads are drifted in." He must have heard her gasp of dismay. His eyes glinted again. "So you better be a good girl. You couldn't make a break for it, if you tried."

"But I *will* try," Judy vowed silently. "I *will* try!"

She said aloud, "Tell me what I should do."

"Sit there." Hugen pointed to the chair where she first found herself. "Answer the questions I'm going to ask you. That's all. It doesn't matter which way you answer—you can suit yourself. Keep an eye on the one who's asking, that's all. You can get the expression. What they want to know. But, like I told you, it doesn't make a great deal of difference. The main thing is to keep up the illusion. You're something from the Spirit World. You're smart enough to catch on to what I mean."

Something from the Spirit World!

Judy suppressed a wild desire to laugh, to throw back her head and burst into peals of merriment. But that would not do. No, that would never do at all.

She must only nod her head in subjection. She must be the good trouper, play the part. Earnestly, unselfishly—something from the Spirit World.

Apparently she convinced the man, for he said, "Now, I'll get them in here. Sit down, and get a set look on your face."

Judy seated herself. She looked straight ahead. Her hands were folded in her lap. She felt certain she thus achieved the "set look."

But there was nothing stiff about her thoughts, her plan of action. Wildly, extravagantly, she plotted. How she would turn the trick on the trickster. How she would bring about his undoing. Above all, how she would clear the way to that door with the big key in the lock.

Hugen was saying quietly, solemnly, "You may come in now."

Footsteps came, shuffling, hesitant. No one spoke a word.

"Now," Judy told herself, "put on your act!"

CHAPTER NINE

MOUSE IN A TRAP

Judy did not once look at any of them, nor at Hugen either. She looked over them, fixing her gaze upon a space above their heads. Nearer they came to where she sat, and still none of them spoke. Finally they all stood in a ragged semi-circle.

"I want them to sit down," Judy thought. "I won't start until they do. I'll get the idea over."

She sat rigidly in the chair, her hands crossed in her lap. Only her eyes moved—slowly, slowly, peering into a world they could not see.

She could sense Hugen's impatience. But he worked to keep up the impression of the master of ceremonies. Having his audience shuffling uneasily was not to his liking.

"Draw up chairs," he said gravely. And in the ensuing shuffle and scraping, Judy could not restrain the wild flutter of hope that soared ever higher within her. It was a little thing. Such a little thing. And yet it was a step in the right direction.

But she made herself sit quietly, staring straight ahead. And she knew that this was not going to be easy. Waves of weariness crept over her ankles, spreading numbly to her knees. She was tired, desperately tired. Physically, she was forced to sit there, relaxed.

No, that was impossible. She must keep herself ready. Her feet must be ready at the right moment to leap to do her bidding. To carry her swiftly to the door. Later, there would be time to sleep. But not now.

Not that the thought of sleep actually came to the girl. And any fear that she might permit her taut nerves to loosen was quickly dispelled when the people were seated before her, the five men and the two women. This was the audience to whom she would play, but it was more than that—more than the projecting of a character, an idea. This audience and she were one. So close, so taut, that Judy could feel them pressing upon her, absorbing her.

The spell would have to be broken. They would not speak first. And Hugen seemed for the moment at a loss.

This was a new experience for Hugen. Or perhaps he was presenting a spirit to this particular group for the first time. Or was it that he was waiting for a sign from Judy?

"I'll give it to him!" Judy laughed deep down in her heart, a laugh they could not take away, nor know existed. She leaned back in the chair and closed her eyes.

"I'll think of a name," she told herself. "A name that they must know, or some of them know. A common, ordinary name." She gave a deep sigh. Let her hands move to the arms of the chair. Her lips moved, silently at first, and then she said the name that came to her, the name of the woman who was mistress of this garage apartment.

"Elizabeth—"

There was a small bustle in the room. Judy's eyes were closed, but she knew they were all looking at Martin, Elizabeth's husband. They were all awed beyond speech, all except Martin.

"My wife," he said, with a gasping of breath. "You heard her?"

Someone said, "Yes. Yes. Listen."

Judy said again, "Elizabeth." And added what came next to her mind. "Elizabeth—is—afraid." She kept her eyes closed, her head back, but the effect of this had been electrical.

"Oh, *she* was afraid, Martin!" It was the woman with the reverent look. "She ran away—!"

The glow of hope soared higher in Judy's throat. So that was why Elizabeth had come back to the Mattis house: because she had been afraid. Perhaps, she had met some of the people gathered here. No, not perhaps, that must have been the case exactly. She had found out about Martin's spirit club, had seen them, and had fled to the big house. Perhaps to tell Freddy. If she had told the blond girl, then Freddy knew what was happening here in the garage. Freddy might send help!

Judy's thought veered. First of all Elizabeth would not tell Freddy. Why Judy was so certain about this, she could not tell. But she was sure Elizabeth would keep Martin's secret, protect him, even while his meandering along ghostly trails was so to her distaste. So Freddy would not know. And, even if she did, how could she guess Judy's plight? Or do anything to help her?

There was no one to help Judy except herself. First, help herself to get out of here, and then reach Grace Doyle. Before it was too late!

How her mind whirled! The space of time covered was such a few seconds, while the woman murmured to Martin, while Martin gasped and while Hugen brought them to attention.

He said, "Wait. There will be more." And Judy heard a kind of admiration in his metallic voice. He had not expected such a performance even from his seasoned actress.

Judy thought, "I should say there will be more!" But she permitted herself a long-drawn-out sigh. "Poor Elizabeth," she said. "Her feet hurt her." She had thought of the flat slippers, toeing in.

"That they do," Martin confided to one of the others. "Why, only last night—"

One of the men cut in. "Let her get done with you, Martin. The rest of us want something told us, too."

"Yes, time is precious." This was the man with the shock of hair. "Let us wait. Listen. She's going to speak again."

Judy obliged him. "She is not—coming back—to-night," she said slowly. "Poor Elizabeth. But she will not be cold. No, not cold. She is high, high in a lonely place."

Martin tried to hold his peace but could not. "The porch," he blurted. "They put her on the porch. I saw the lights in there."

This, Judy knew, was as far as she dared to go in her statements—with certainty. It was also as far as she *meant* to go. She had no intention of making the wild, disjointed predictions that Hugen had suggested. To do that would be to prey upon the credence of these poor, foolish souls—to predict or interpret their destiny. Nor was it necessary to try any such thing. She had won them—completely. She was never more sure of an audience—and never more eager to be done with the play.

She took her cue from the word *lights*. It was as good as any.

But first of all, she let her eyelids flutter, weakly, wearily. "Lights," she breathed. "There are the lights."

It could mean anything, and perhaps some of them drew their own chosen conclusion. Judy was looking straight ahead. Hugen was sitting there, where he had been before. Martin was at his right. By a movement of her head, Judy was able to see the rest of them, leaning forward, scarcely breathing, waiting to learn which one would receive the forthcoming "message."

They did not dream it was to come to all of them–all, perhaps, except Hugen.

"Lights," Judy repeated, and let the word trail off in a small gasp. It was not difficult for her to give way to fear, to conjure up the feeling of terror. If she failed the future for her was rimmed with danger. But she must not fail. She must make these people afraid. "Oh the lights are coming!" she quavered in a pitiful wail "The lights. Be careful of the lights!"

There was an agitated murmur, and it grew in volume. A chair was pushed backward. The man with the cap said, "What lights? What lights are you talking about?"

"From the–East," the girl said. "East, and South."

She had spoken at random. It did not matter where the lights came from. But the man with the scar interpreted it swiftly: "That's the direction of town," he said hoarsely. "D'you think–?"

"Who could know?" Hugen cut in shortly. "Nothing definite has been said. *Be careful now!*"

But he was not talking to the *man,* he was aiming a warning at Judy. She was the one who must be careful: Keep to her prescribed role; pacify these people; lead them on.

Hugen was talking to them. "You came across the lake. How could anybody know? Wait, now. You'll get it *straight!*"

Straight! Yes, they would get it straight.

Judy let herself shudder. And that was not difficult. Her hands came up to her face. "Oh, the lights are so bright," she said. "They hurt my eyes."

And now she knew that the word she had chosen could not have been better. The yellow light. The *lamp*. She would get them to turn it out, but not right away.

The woman with the hollow cheeks said, "The poor thing. I wish I hadn't come. Frank said I should stay at home. But I wouldn't listen."

Martin snapped, "Be quiet. You won't get a chance like this again. You wanted me to call you."

"Yes. But I didn't know—"

Hugen cried, "Quiet!" Silence settled, an uneasy silence. Judy heard one of the men cough uncomfortably.

She kept her hands before her face. "I'm choking," she said slowly. "I feel—that I am choking!" Her hands came down. She stared straight at a spot five inches above Hugen's eyes, blazing their warning. His lips were moving, too, forming words, but Judy was unaware of him. Her hands went to her throat. "They are too close to me!" she said. "I cannot see the things. I cannot hear!" She appealed to some invisible power, keeping her eyes on the gilded photograph of the woman in the high-necked gown. "Tell them I cannot hear," she moaned.

Something was wrong. Hugen knew this, but did

not know what it was. Even if he knew, he was powerless to offer any resistance. The "spirit" who had been mesmerized from the lake had spoken, and that was command enough for the others.

"We're too close," Martin said unnecessarily. "We've got to move back."

The voices rose, and the chairs went back against the wall. Hugen obeyed with the others, but a moment after they had all seated themselves, he remained standing, forcing himself into Judy's line of vision. "This is better," he said. "Now we can go on—*as we had planned.*"

Judy looked at him, and through him. "Not as we had planned," she thought. "Not at all!"

The silence settled, all of them waiting for her to speak. She took refuge in another deep sigh, and returned to her chosen subject.

"The lights," she said softly. "You cannot see them. But they are there. They are coming—closer, closer!" She thought, "Forget about the yellow lamp, it's working this way. Perfectly!"

"Golly," the man with the cap gasped. "I think I'll hit for the lake."

Judy went on, letting her eyes grow wider, wider. "They are coming closer. Oh, be careful! Be careful! I am afraid! Oh, I am afraid!" Her voice rose, higher, higher in terror. "*I am afraid!*" she cried, and the dismal wail beat against the walls of the room.

Hugen tried to calm the group, tried to send another oblique warning to the girl who was behaving so outrageously. But Hugen's voice did not carry in the surge that followed. Judy had spun a web of terror over their heads, so fine a thread that they could not define it. They were lost, confused; above all, they were afraid.

She got slowly to her feet. Her eyes remained straight ahead.

"There," she said, pointing with a rigid dramatic finger. "The lights will come from—there." She turned, stiffly, her arm still extended, toward the right —toward the archway. That was the farthest point from the door. "There," she murmured so gently they had to strain their ears to hear. "That is the way. I cannot—I cannot—!"

It did not make sense. The guess, *East* and *South*, which had been interpreted to mean the direction of the city, could not score again. But now, nothing needed to make sense. They were gripped in the spell. All except Hugen. He was sitting forward on his chair, glaring at her with white-hot fury.

Judy wanted to run now, at once. But first she must make the way definitely clear. The key had to be turned in the lock. Then she could open the door at her left. It was not far from her. She had edged back a little from the chair. Four, maybe five steps would bring her to the lock. Her lips parted suddenly in a piteous cry:

"Oh, look!" she pleaded miserably. "Look—and you

will see!"

They looked, all of them—even Hugen—to the right.

And the girl whirled and made the dash toward the door. Her hands found the key. She turned it.

They were watching her now, dazed, still in a frozen state of terror. But they must sense that something was definitely wrong. Hugen knew. And his voice was a bellow of rage. He called out something, and Judy heard his chair overturning as he surged forward. Martin had risen, too. Judy learned, in the next moment, that it was Martin. Hugen collided with him. That was how Hugen happened to be stopped, how the extra, precious moments were given the girl. And the need for time was desperate.

The key did not give easily, or Judy's hands were aching, numb. But it turned at last—and the door opened. She was on the other side of it, closing it after her.

In the split second after she had again turned the key, on the safe side of the door, she heard Hugen's fists pounding. She heard his demanding cry: "Open that door! Do you hear me? Open that door!"

The others present were in a state of wild confusion. Things had taken too sudden a turn for them to come to a clear understanding. Perhaps they would never know what had actually happened. Hugen could not admit that the "spirit" which had so recently been in their midst was not a genuine visitation from the "so-called dead." He would have to explain that very earthly exit Judy had made—perhaps by explaining that the lake had called back its own. That was Hugen's worry. Or, maybe, it was Martin's.

Judy did not know, or care, whose worry it was. Standing on the other side of the door, while the tumult and voices raised a din in the room, she leaned weakly against a wall. It was dark, absolutely dark, where she was. She had no idea which way to turn. She did not know how far she was from the driveway which led toward the house.

As she hesitated there, her weakness was what saved her from serious hurt. For her hand found a railing that slanted down.

Stairs! She bent forward, ran her fingers over the smooth wood. It was a railing and it went down sharply. She was at the head of a flight of stairs.

Gripping the rail, she slid her right foot along, over the edge, then down. One step, another and another. So many steps. The garage apartment must be on the second floor. But, then, of course it must be. Where else could it be?

She went down, and down.

There was a noticeable drop in the temperature. The air became more and more cold as the girl put greater distance between herself and the group in the room above. Where would she find herself when she reached the bottom of the steps? At a door leading to the driveway? That was what she hoped. From the driveway, she could go to the main highway. Hugen said it was drifted full, so there could be no traffic. But perhaps Hugen had said that to frighten her, to induce her to obey him. Even if it were true, there was still—the lake. The rest of them had come that way. So they said. They would return that way, if their story was true. But it was a big lake. If they could manage it, so could she. She would wait until the way was clear, and then go ahead.

But now?

She noticed that the voices overhead had stopped abruptly. The tumult had risen to a kind of peak or crescendo, and then, suddenly, it was followed by a quiet that was worse.

They were following her! Judy knew that surely. Following her by another way, a way of which she could not know.

She forced herself to picture the place where she was, and to imagine the way the others might have gone. These were the inside stairs. There were probably outside stairs, giving down immediately to the driveway.

It was possible, then, that she was in the garage. Not only possible: it was so. Her hands touched a door, found the knob. She opened it and the smell of gasoline, of oil, was unmistakable.

If only, the girl thought frantically, *if only there were a light!* So that she might hide, before Hugen could come. Because he would come, and find her. Martin would show him the way, if he did not already know the way. Perhaps Hugen would tell him the truth. But, no, he would not dare to do that. They would recognize him for the impostor that he was. Hugen was smart. He had to be smart, to dupe them as he had done. He would think up some plausible explanation for the hasty disappearance of his "spirit." He would, perhaps, bring her back to that upstairs room. The meeting would continue in session.

And then? The men, the women would depart. But she—Judy?

Thinking of her probable fate, the girl could not suppress the moan that escaped from her lips. She was overcome with a weariness of mind and body. There was no gleam of hope, nothing to guide her now. She was spent, incapable of thought, of motion.

And yet, when the sounds materialized out of the night, Judy discovered a still deeper reservoir of strength upon which she had not as yet drawn. Fear, rekindled, lighted the spark anew, the will to fight back, the will to survive.

They were approaching the garage. Hugen and the others. They had a flashlight, for a quick, sharp gleam came piercing through a glass partition, high over the girl's head. It was more like a pinprick of light. And then a hand touched the wide door under the glass.

They were outside the garage, but they were not hurrying to enter. Judy wondered why.

Because the garage doors must face the house!

A Gleam of Light Shone Through the Garage Door

Because a gleam of light could be seen—would be investigated. Martin had no wish to bring the attention of the Mattis household upon his doings with Hugen. And Hugen was, perhaps, most willing to comply. He, also, had no relish of discovery.

So the light came again, a faint gleam over the girl's head. But this time she was ready to avail herself of what it afforded, the glimpse of the three-door garage.

Two cars were in it. A big sedan was nearest to her. Judy stood close to the left, front fender.

She put her hand out, guiding herself around the machine. Her knee touched the front bumper, and then she paused again. She heard a chain rattling—the scrape of a door.

They were coming in. Right into the garage! She must hide. Not in the sedan. She dared not risk going back there again. If the light were turned on, she would be directly in front—in full view of all of them.

She heard the voices. Martin was saying, "Maybe that was the way it should be."

Hugen said, "And maybe not. We have to find out."

So Martin still believed she was a spirit! She had fled through a door as any ordinary mortal might have done, but he still cloaked her with unknown and mysterious power. Because of Elizabeth, because of what she had told him of his wife.

But Hugen meant to trail her down. Hugen meant to see to it that his other customers had their money's worth.

The light came on, hitting the ceiling. Judy cringed under it, turned away, toward the wall which the car was facing. She had a glimpse of the long, massive poles ranged against the wall, along the floor—black and red. And the great roll of cloth. It was canvas. It had been there for a long time, for years, the wood and the cloth. Assembled, it would be an ice boat. But now?

The canvas seemed to be wound around with a small opening showing darkly. It could not be large enough for her to crawl into, and yet that was what she must do. Like a mouse, a mouse which made itself little and flat and slid under a door.

Again, discreetly, the flashlight hit the ceiling. Hugen said, "Don't turn on the garage light, Martin."

"Don't you worry," Martin said staunchly. "I wouldn't."

Judy was close to the roll of canvas. She bent and touched it. Her fingers groped inside what she had thought was the open space. But it did not open. It was solid. The heavy cloth was wound around something, she did not know what. But there was a space behind the roll. Against the wall. Judy half fell, half slid into the place. She felt the canvas move away slightly, and then move back. She was hemmed in close to the wall, a rough cement that touched one cheek harshly. But she was hidden. The pressure of the canvas over her told her that she was hidden.

She could not see the flashlight when it was turned on again, for her eyes could not move upward. She could only look along the floor. The wheels of the car showed in the beam—and presently men's feet: Hugen's worn-over shoes and Martin's. The stout, high-laced shoes must be Martin's, she thought vaguely. She had never noticed particularly before.

But there were no other persons coming into the garage. Judy was certain she had heard more than Hugen and Martin talking. Where, then, were the others? Waiting outside? Making sure the way was clear?

Hugen cried, "We've got her now. She couldn't get out of here!"

And Martin said, "I wouldn't be too sure. I don't see anything."

From somewhere—far away, it seemed—a woman called, "Martin!" The woman with the splash of rouge on her face, Judy guessed. And she was frightened.

For the fraction of a moment, the light fell over the canvas, across the cement floor, then soared again. Martin said, "What's the matter?"

"Look out! We're going!"

A man's voice came, hoarsely: "Somebody's coming!" Then, nearer: "Light the way up the inside stairs!"

They all drew away, toward the stairs down which Judy had come. Judy could hear their muffled footsteps going upward, farther and farther away. At last a door banged shut, and she knew they had all gone into the upstairs apartment.

She was left alone. She had not been discovered in her hiding place back of the canvas.

It took some time for her to realize that she had been successful in her little plan. Hugen was gone. The men and the two women were gone. Someone had come and frightened them into taking flight.

Martin must be left alone, of course. But Martin was content to drop the search for her. As far as Martin was concerned, she was the "spirit" and she had returned to the lake in the mysterious way she had come.

She was free—free to come out, free to strike out for the highway. Because the last thing she thought of doing was to head for the lake—not unless there was no other way. She dared not risk meeting Hugen!

But, first of all, she must risk discovery by coming out from her hiding place.

Judy leaned back against the wall, braced herself, and slowly, painfully, brought her hands upward to press against the heavy roll of cloth. It gave slightly, as though she had dented the material, but the weight that pressed down against her did not lessen. She tried again, exerting all the strength she could summon. The result was the same. The *cloth* pressed inward, but the great *roll itself* did not give in the slightest degree.

Panic struck the girl, all the more terrifying because

release was so near. Was she hemmed in, helplessly caught? It could not be! She had managed to hide in this space, so there surely must be a way out.

She tried again, and again. It was no use. The long poles must have slid and locked in some way, bearing upon the canvas. She was caught: trapped.

Weak from her futile exertions, she gave in, leaning back. A sob rose in her throat. But quickly she drew her lips together. Had she heard a sound on the steps? Or was it only the dull hammering in her head?

It was footsteps, coming nearer. Coming down the inside stairway, as she had come!

Had Hugen returned? Would she be discovered, caught here in her neat trap?

Stiffly, forcing her ears to tell what her eyes could not see, Judy waited for what might be in store for her.

CHAPTER TEN

LATE ARRIVAL

Whoever was coming, nearer and nearer, was walking stiffly, or was wearing heavy shoes. Judy remembered Martin's shoes—the high-laced workman's boots. Yes, it must be Martin. Who else could it be? The others had fled, and Hugen must have fled with them.

The footfalls ceased. The unseen person had reached the bottom of the inside steps. Judy heard the tinkle—probably of keys—and heard a man's voice muttering, "No, it's gone. Must have mislaid it." It was Martin, the girl was certain now. He went on muttering to himself; "And they dropped the other one in the snow. Not a chance of finding it tonight." The jangle of the keys died away abruptly. They had been thrust, perhaps, into the man's pocket.

There came the sound of wood scraping on wood. "Got to lock it from the inside," Martin grumbled.

He was going to lock the door. Judy guessed that a wooden bar was about to be slipped into place. If that were all, it would be simple for her to open the door again, after Martin had gone. Because she could never make her escape by going back the way she had come here, up the inside stairway to the apartment overhead.

Escape! she thought crazily, and almost laughed—with utter hopelessness. How could she escape, hemmed in here as she was? What did it matter how many doors Martin bolted or locked?

But if she were to cry out, to let the old man know she was here? Martin might be greatly surprised to see his "spirit" in such an earthbound predicament, but Judy felt certain he would do her no harm. Martin might blunder in Hugen's footsteps, but he was not—she felt her heart leap—*a murderer!*

A gleam of light twisted close over the floor, then lifted. Martin had picked up the flash, and then set it down to guide him more surely. He was muttering to himself, "I don't understand it!" A fogged and almost pathetic voice, a voice that decided the girl on the instant.

"I'll let him know I'm here!" she thought. "I have to. There's no other way out—unless he *helps* me out!"

She drew a deep breath. Her lips, stiff and cold, were even slightly open to speak, but the words were suddenly brushed away, lost in the uproar that reverberated in the big, bleak room.

Someone was pounding on the garage door. From the outside, a man's voice was calling, "Wait a minute. Let me in!"

Martin exploded softly. "Well—!" And, after a short pause. "Who is it? Who's there?"

He knew it was not Hugen, nor any of the other men who had been here before. It had to be a stranger.

"Fergussen," the man said. "Jimmy Fergussen."

"Fergussen?" Martin repeated, and then seemed to come alive. "Y'mean, Jimmy Fergussen, the fellow that—!"

The man outside was pounding impatiently. Judy thought he said, "That's me. Open the door. I want to talk to you."

"Sure, Mister," Martin said, and broke off. "Captain,—sure!"

The bolt must have been lifted again. Judy heard it, and the stamping sound of shoes on hard cement, but she was recalling the name the man had given. *Captain Jimmy Fergussen.* He was somebody important, she was sure. But it was difficult to remember because of her weariness, and the cold, and her discomfort.

The door of the garage swung open. The stamping sound was louder and the late arrival said, "Golly, you keep it cold here!"

Judy heard the old man chuckle for the first time. It was a hearty, crusty sound. "We take what we can get," he said, and added quickly, "Come on in. Come on in. You're not used to this weather yet."

"Give me time," Jimmy Fergussen said, and the rich deep quality of his voice seemed to warm the place, to dispel the shreds of gloom and doubt.

Martin closed the door. While it was still scraping,

he said loudly, "I never thought to see you out here, Mister. They had a party in town for you tonight, didn't they?"

"Yes, they did. But the person I wanted most of all to see wasn't there. *That's* why I came out here."

Judy knew the truth then. She had known all along, really. But she remembered the story of Jimmy Fergussen: the incredible deeds of daring he had done in the air war. This was his home town, the town where Freddy lived. Judy could not reconcile the Mattis house as being a part of the town. It was too much like a gloomy fortress, aloof, remote.

The young man was saying more: "I saw a number of people out here. Thought maybe it was a party. Everything was dark in the big house."

Martin must have been smiling, but he sobered quickly. "People?" he said. "Oh, yes. Yes, there were some—people here."

"I came barging through the snow, flashing my light. It looked as though I scared 'em away." As he said it, the words were a question. He must have found the manner of the "people's" leave-taking most unusual. Because Hugen and the others were afraid of being discovered. Perhaps they thought the man represented the police.

Martin coughed. "Guess they were in a hurry," he said. "It's a bad night to be out."

"Bad night is right! My car's down about a mile. I walked the rest of the way." There came a flat, slapping sound, as though stout leather gloves were being clapped together. "I suppose you're the caretaker?"

"Y-Yes," Martin said. "Yes, I'm the caretaker. Live upstairs. The name's Brooks. Martin Brooks."

"You suppose we could go on up, Martin? I'm chilled to the bone—and I might have to ask you for a bunk tonight. Too late to make my appearance at the house."

"Bunk—here?" Martin said, with a shade of uncertainty, which he quickly righted. "Why, yes. Sure, you could."

Abruptly Judy became conscious of her own need. She had been listening intently, puzzling over the sudden appearance here of the hero—and wasting time. Why was she hesitating? Why didn't she shout out to them? There was nothing to fear from Captain Fergussen, nor from Martin. Her head ached. Her back ached. She was so cold, so drearily cold.

She opened her lips and called out. But her voice sounded strange, small in the emptiness.

"Help me! Please—help me!"

It was Jimmy Fergussen who cried, abruptly sharp, "What was that?" There was a slight pause. "Wait, Martin!"

Silence.

Judy mustered all her strength. "Help!" Her voice was louder, higher. "Help me out of here!"

Martin gasped, "It's the—it's the—!" But Jimmy Fergussen cut in, "It's a girl! There's a girl in here!"

He called out, "Where are you?"

"Back—of the canvas."

Martin was muttering something about not understanding, but the young man was urging him to action. "Where's the canvas? Help me locate it. Come on, man. Wake up!"

Martin said dully, "She went away. But she came back. She came back again."

"All right,"—impatiently—"where's that canvas now?"

The two were nearer, coming in front of the car, coming to where Judy was hemmed in. Martin said, "That's it," in a whisper of awe, as though he were drawing back. He must be drawing back, for Jimmy Fergussen said shortly, "Here, hold my flashlight!"

Gratefully Judy felt the pressing weight lightening. Hands, strong, yet gentle, lifted her. And then, for the second time that strange, eventful night, she lapsed into unconsciousness and forgetfulness.

But her waking was not fraught with fear, like the previous time when she had lost consciousness in the snow. She had been a victim of terror then. Martin had loomed so suddenly before her, his arms outspread. When she awoke this time, it was different. The feeling of having reached a friendly haven lingered in her mind, even though she found her eyes still heavy-lidded. With a warm sense of well-being she heard the murmur of the men's voices. She was not certain, at once, who the men were. But they were friends. At long last she was confident that she was in the hands of friends.

Something pressed close around her, comfortably soft and warm. Someone lifted a cup to her lips with something hot. Obediently, she opened her mouth and sipped the liquid.

Then she opened her eyes and saw the young man who was holding the cup.

"That's better," he said. "Come on, drink some more like a good girl."

It was a pleasure to obey him. Judy drained the cup.

She was sitting in the same chair she had occupied before, when the row of intense faces had been lined before her. But now a thick quilt was about her and the chair had been moved. She was on the other side of the archway, in the dining-room, in front of a bright stove. Her feet were propped on a low stool, close to the warmth of the fire. And the face before her was that of Captain Jimmy Fergussen. Judy remembered that well enough.

His eyes were looking down at her with a mixture of approval and curiosity, greenish-blue eyes under heavy dark brows, set in a bony, high-cheeked face. A lock of rust-brown hair trailed down over his forehead—curly hair, valiantly smoothed down but irrepressible. At first glance, the lock seemed to extend down toward one lean cheek. But Judy knew better. That penciled line would never be erased. That was a mark he would always carry, a scar. Wide lips were smiling, showing even, strong teeth.

The man said, "Feel better?"

"Oh, yes!" Judy told him fervently. "I don't know how to tha—"

"Don't try," he advised. He was holding the empty cup, and looking toward a lighted door beyond. The kitchen, Judy saw, with an oilcloth-covered table showing. He called out, "Martin. Oh, Martin—"

The old man came into view, slowly. His eyes looked at the two of them—eyes that Judy had remembered because they bulged so whitely. But there was nothing terrifying in the man now. Martin's shoulders were slightly bent, the girl observed. He was unsure of himself, of them.

He said, "Yes, sir?"

"Could we have a refill?" Jimmy Fergussen held out the cup. His arm crossed over in front of Judy, an arm in a thick, dark brown overcoat. "Maybe I'll take another myself."

Martin said again, "Yes, sir. I got plenty. I got another teapot full."

He came in, walking as widely in front of the girl as possible, and took the cup from the man. Almost gingerly, trying not to look at her, he stepped away, back to the kitchen.

Jimmy Fergussen might not know, but Judy understood the conflict that raged in the old man's breast. Or she partly understood it.

Martin Came in Carrying the Teapot

Martin's "spirit" was only a girl, a girl who did not take form from the lake or disappear into nothingness. She was quite human, for she had hidden behind the roll of canvas, she was chilled and numb, she relished the cheer of a cup of tea.

Jimmy Fergussen's eyes were also on the old man, watching him as he moved past the open door. And then he and Judy exchanged a quick glance that covered miles of understanding, and yet left marks along the way, the hundred and one stops, just so many bursting questions.

The young man said, "You want to tell me something about it? How Martin happens to be calling you a 'spirit'?"

"He—he doesn't—any more, does he?" Judy asked softly.

"No." A smile tugged at one corner of the young man's mouth. "Not any more. But it took some convincing." He reached for a chair, one of the four around a square table, and brought it nearer. "Too close to the stove?" he asked.

"No. It feels wonderful."

"Good." He sat down, leaning back, looking toward the kitchen. Martin came in with a tray. On it were two cups and the tea pot. He set it on the table and almost beat a retreat into the kitchen.

One of the young man's eyebrows lifted at the hasty back, but he did not call out to the old man. He poured the tea, gave Judy a cup, served himself.

He said, "Well—?"

"I," Judy hesitated, "I don't know where to begin."

"How about the *beginning?*" The young man suggested and applied himself to his steaming cup.

What had been the beginning? It went back so far —to this afternoon; no, it was yesterday afternoon. When Dora Brit had asked her to return the beautiful gown to a girl named Frederica Hammond. That hoodoo costume had been the beginning—too far back. Then, the visit with the Doyle sisters, with Grace and Marion. That, also, was too distant.

Grace Doyle. Thinking of Grace, Judy put down her cup, hastily, so that some of the drops that were left splashed out on the saucer.

Jimmy Fergussen leaned forward. He said again, his voice deeper, "Well—?"

"I have to leave this house," Judy told him urgently. "I have to get back to the city. There's something I—"

She would have risen. Her hands were ready to toss aside the folds of the quilt. But Jimmy Fergussen held her arm, pushed her gently but firmly back into the chair.

"In good time," he said. "But not yet. You're not ready—and I'm not ready."

"But, Captain Fergussen—!"

"My friends call me Jimmy."

"All right,—Jimmy." Judy smiled ghostily. But she smiled. The man's teeth flashed in an appreciative smile. "That's much better," he said.

"But, this is important," Judy persisted. "Really important. A number of people are concerned—"

"In the house?" Jimmy asked.

"Yes. In the house." Neither said the *Mattis house*, but to Judy it was the only house to be considered, then. And Jimmy Fergussen was also interested in someone there. What was it he had said? When he first came into the garage? There had been a celebration for him, but the one he had wanted most to see had not been present. That was why he was here now!

Judy shook her head to clear the cobwebs from it. What did it matter why he was here? His coming had been a rare stroke of luck for her. If Martin had been the one to discover her, alone, he might not have had the wit to release her from her prison behind the canvas. He might not have believed that she was a girl, only a helpless girl of flesh and blood. But Jimmy had been the one to find her, to bring her back to a sense of rightness. It was in Jimmy Fergussen that she must confide, fully.

But that nagging sense of moments flying past, being wasted, bothered her. Now, they were all asleep in the Mattis house. Jimmy had said it was dark. That was why he had come here, to the garage. There was no harm brewing in the Mattis house at this moment. Or was there? Had Garth Frazer succeeded in inducing Myrta to take the medicine which no doctor had prescribed? Myrta must have been very upset after the session with Elizabeth. She might have found it impossible to relax. The little drawer in her dresser was not locked. She could easily—

Jimmy's voice broke in: "I wish you'd let me in on it. Two heads are better than one, Judy."

Judy! Jimmy knew her. But he was not like the group that had clustered here not so long ago, the people who looked upon her as a ghostly being.

Judy said, "You know me?" but it was not important. Her mind was on Freddy, on Myrta, and on Garth Frazer.

She heard the young man say, "I didn't at first. But when I bathed your face, to help you come to, I looked again—and there you were!"

He was grinning at her. And she had to grin back. Martin, in the kitchen, made a sudden movement, perhaps stepped backward and touched a chair. Judy had forgotten about Martin, there were so many other things to think about—things so much more important. Her hand went to her head, pushing at the curls that seemed too heavy for comfort.

"Believe it or not," Jimmy said confidentially, "I have my troubles, too." He was serious now.

Judy looked swiftly into his face. "Yes?" she breathed.

"Yes. And I was thinking, maybe, if we started with mine, we might work together a little better. Perhaps you can help me—if you've been in the house."

"Why, yes," Judy said quickly. "I've been in the

house."

Jimmy went on, "Martin's told me she's there. But he's tight-mouthed about the thing I want most of all to know." Again, there came a sound from the kitchen. The old man was listening, of course. But Jimmy went on, "It concerns a girl, Frederica Hammond. Do you know her?"

The question was pointless, spoken as Judy gasped with surprise. Jimmy said, "I see that you do."

"Oh, yes. Yes, I know Freddy. It was—because of Freddy that I wanted to get away."

The young man leaned forward. "She's in trouble?"

"I think so." *Trust him,* ran her thought. *Tell him the truth.* "I know she's in trouble, Jimmy."

"That's what Miss Doyle told me."

Judy drew in her breath sharply. "Miss—Doyle? You know them, too? The Doyles?"

"I met Miss Marion this evening," Jimmy told her. "When Freddy didn't show up at the banquet, I broke away as soon as I could. I didn't have time to call Freddy before, came straight from the train, but I looked her up as soon as I was free. Miss Marion told me where she was. I got the impression Freddy was in trouble."

Judy could only say slowly, "So you were there, too."

"She told me of your visit," Jimmy went on, with a gleam in his eyes. "So, when I saw you here, I wasn't too surprised." He hastily amended, "That it was *you,* I mean. But the way you looked, crammed back of that pile of junk, that was bad!"

Judy confessed weakly that it had been rather bad.

"If that was the way they treated their guests at the Mattis house," Jimmy resumed grimly, "I was pretty sure that Miss Doyle had been right. I thought you and I should pool our resources, so to speak. But, first of all, you had to wake up, get warm."

"I—I'm warm now." She glanced about the room. "Wh—What time is it?"

Jimmy consulted his wrist watch. "Three-twenty," he said, and added, "A.M." as though Judy might have asked that, too.

The girl laughed shakily. "Not exactly the time to call on them," she said.

"That's it," Jimmy said. His mouth turned into a hard straight line. His eyes lowered, but a dagger of determination snapped through. This was another Jimmy Fergussen—*Captain Fergussen.* He said, "Unless Fred's in trouble. Unless you can make me sure she's all right. If she isn't—time would be no object."

"Oh, I think she's all right," Judy told him earnestly. "She's all right—*now.* It's nothing—definite. Nothing you can lay your hands on." She groped for words, words to explain the horror that hung over the blond girl's head. "It's—it's the whole house, Jimmy. Most of all it's Garth Frazer—"

"Who's Garth Frazer?"

"A—a kind of an uncle, I guess. He's got everybody

doing as he says. Freddy's afraid that—"

Martin came into the open door just then. Judy saw him, and was reminded of her arrival at the Mattis house. Disregarding the old man, she said in a rush:

"The place is guarded, Jimmy. When I got off the bus, Martin was back of one of the big urns in front of the house. He chased me. I think it was because he thought I was his 'spirit of the lake.' But, just the same, the place is guarded. Freddy is about the same as a prisoner—"

She paused, because Martin was staring at her so dully, because she heard him give a low groan. Jimmy said, "Yes? About Freddy?"

Taking a fresh breath, she went on, "Oh, it's so muddled. It's so hard to explain, Jimmy. You almost have to be there. You almost have to see them. And this Garth Frazer. And he isn't the only one—"

Judy paused. She was going to tell him more about Myrta Mattis, whom Freddy loved, and who was coming to have a real affection for the niece she had neglected too long. She was going to tell him about Cilla Keene, whom she had not seen, about Harris Morley, all of them, who seemed bent upon prolonging Myrta's illness, stifling Freddy's valiant effort to help the woman.

"Who else is there?"

Judy heard the cool, brittle words which emerged from the next room, where Judy had escaped to the inner stairs. But this speaker was not near that door. It was another door, the door which led to the outside stairs. Judy had not noticed it. But she had known that it must be there, when Hugen and the others had come down. She knew it was there now, and that Cilla Keene had entered that way. Because, though she had never seen Myrta Mattis's daughter, Judy would not forget her voice. She leaned back in her chair, staring through the archway. The young man had turned, and his gaze followed hers. They saw the woman coming toward them—tall, large boned. Her face had a creamy pallor; the outstanding feature was a full, sulky mouth. She was not as dark as Myrta, not as beautiful. But you would not look away from her. You would look at her again.

Judy not only looked, she stared. At the brown hair smooth on the arrogant head, the splash of orange, yellow and brown that was the dress Cilla wore under her fur coat. The dress was stained darkly at the hem, and the woman's shoes must be soaked through. Judy thought, "She came from the house, through the snow. It must be deep."

Jimmy Fergussen had risen. Judy knew that he was standing, a bulwark against any foe, but still she found no answer ready for Cilla's question, which surely had been aimed at her.

The woman came nearer. She said, again, "Well, what is Freddy so frightened about? Garth Frazer isn't the only one, you say. *Who else?*"

Judy heard Martin. He coughed huskily, as though to draw their attention. Or Judy's attention. But Judy did not turn toward him. She was looking at Cilla Keene. She thought, "Are the others awake in the house? Why is Cilla here? How, oh, how is this all going to end?"

CHAPTER ELEVEN

THE WAY BACK

It was Jimmy Fergussen who broke the silence that blanketed the dining-room. He said, with a calm that did not deceive Judy, "You know the lady, Judy?"

Judy nodded, and when the woman gave a gasp of astonishment, she felt a small imp of pleasure dance in her heart. The girl knew she was about to be recognized as a famous person still another time, and thought that sometimes it was fun. Where women like Cilla Keene were concerned—women to whom names and numbers meant so much—people meant so little.

"You can't be Judy Garland!" was the way she put it.

"I'm afraid so," Judy said demurely.

Cilla came in, swept in, despite her snow-bedraggled frock. She looked searchingly at the girl in the chair. The glance reduced the warm quilt to a sorry thing, patched and worn. It chilled the heat that had come from the stove. "I don't believe it," she said flatly.

Jimmy said to Judy, "Does it matter?" With his back to Cilla, he asked, "Who is she?"

"Her name is Cilla," Judy told him. "She's Mrs. Mattis's daughter."

Jimmy said, rather blankly, "Oh."

It was more than Cilla could endure. "What are you two doing here?" she demanded hotly. "I want an explanation of this!" She looked about, toward the kitchen. "Martin!" she called. "Martin, come here!"

The old man came, shuffling wearily in his heavy shoes. Judy thought suddenly, "He's old. And he's tired, and so disappointed."

But Martin was more than old and tired and disappointed. He was worried, greatly worried—as Judy was soon to discover.

Though he came at Cilla's bidding, it was toward Jimmy Fergussen that Martin's eyes went in a kind of pleading way, as though begging him to excuse Cilla Keene.

"Why?" Judy asked herself. And then she guessed the truth. It was because Cilla had not known who Captain Jimmy was. She did not live here, now, in the Mattis house. She had not yet seen the local hero's picture in the paper, or she would have been humbler in her attitude. Where Cilla had come from, Judy did not know—nor particularly care. But, somehow, she seemed to recall that it must be from some distance away, because Cilla had complained at one time or another of being very tired from the trip.

Very tired. Judy realized that she, herself, was very tired. The night was almost over. The long, long night, that trailed itself through the strange, dark hours, where people moved like unreal shadows—

people who so craved riches that they would cunningly persuade a sick woman to poison herself, or let herself be poisoned. People who braved the fury of a storm to gather in an apartment over a garage, because an old caretaker had told them a spirit had materialized out of frozen Lake Oleen. People who were afraid, afraid, each in his own warped way.

All except Jimmy and herself—and Freddy. Perhaps Myrta was not afraid. But surely she must be, and Cilla must be. But why had she come here, at this hour?

Judy's head felt numb as though not a part of her. She could not direct her thoughts in a definite channel. Not then. She thought idly, "What does it matter? What sense is there in any of this? I don't belong here!"

But she *was* here. She had *come* here, made herself a part of the strangeness and the fear.

She saw Martin coming nearer, nearer to where Cilla stood in the archway. But he appeared to move so slowly—why had it taken Martin so long to come such a little way? Perhaps Judy's thoughts, despite her mental numbness, had wandered widely. Martin was standing near Cilla, and she was saying, "What is the meaning of this, Martin? What are these two doing here?"

The old man looked uneasily at Jimmy Fergussen, at Judy. Jimmy came to his rescue.

"We just dropped in on him," he explained easily.

"The house was dark, so we came here."

Cilla raised her head again. "Oh, the house was dark. Do you mean you wished to see somebody—at the house?" Her tone said, "When you could only expect to get into a place like this."

Jimmy nodded. "That's right," he said. "We wished to see somebody at the house. But, by the time we forced our way through the drifts, it was pretty late."

Cilla snorted. She turned away from him, back to Martin. "What were those people doing out in front of the garage?" she demanded. "I saw them out there, flashing a light."

Martin's mouth opened, but he made no sound. Cilla went on, "Speak, man. First it's Elizabeth, rushing up the stairs, screaming her head off. Scaring us all half to death. Then, when I think I'll get a little sleep, you start flashing lights out here. I want to know what's going on!"

Judy thought, "I'll have to give her credit for some spunk. Coming out here alone." There came an addition, not so gentle: "*If* Cilla came alone."

But now Judy knew why Martin looked so worried. He had assumed that everyone in the house must be asleep—that the way was clear. But Cilla had seen the lights—and the people. And Martin had wanted desperately to keep the meeting with Hugen and the others a secret.

Jimmy Fergussen said flatly, "What people?" He looked at Martin. "Maybe she means that car that got stuck. The folks that asked if we could pull them out?"

The mists of weariness were clouding Judy's thoughts, but not so darkly that she did not perceive Jimmy's quick deception. He had come neatly to Martin's aid. Did Jimmy know of the secret meeting? Had Martin told him? Judy doubted it. Martin would not have had time, nor would he want to. As Judy remembered, all Martin had admitted was that there had been "some people here." Because it had been so cold, they had "hurried away." But Jimmy had seen them, too. He had seen the way they must have scuttled toward the lake, avoiding him.

It was nothing at all the way Jimmy put it, "folks" asking for a lift. To put it that way gave the impression that nothing unusual had happened. At least it cleared the fear from Martin's eyes, which was what Jimmy had meant to happen. He liked Martin.

Cilla had hoped for something different. She snapped, "If you had the lights out at a decent time, Martin, every Tom, Dick and Harry wouldn't be pounding around here all hours of the night."

Martin murmured, "Yes, ma'am," but the sigh he gave was of deep relief, and the look he sent in Jimmy's direction spoke volumes.

Jimmy corrected her: "We're not *every* Tom, Dick and Harry, ma'am. It was our intention not to call until a reasonable hour, but, if the other members of the house are awake, we might return with you."

Cilla gave a slight gasp, but Jimmy turned to Judy.

"Are you warm enough?" he asked her. His eyes were steady, sending their quiet but unspoken message: *Perhaps we had better not wait longer. Perhaps Freddy needs us now. Perhaps tomorrow may be too late.*

Judy tossed the quilt aside.

"I'm ready—as soon as I get my coat," she said.

Cilla was looking over her head as though she did not exist. She said to Martin, "You'd better come back with me. Elizabeth's moaning so out there on the porch, I can't get any rest. You'll have to calm her."

Judy thought, "That was really why she came out here. To get Martin. To bring him back to the house."

Martin shuffled uneasily. Cilla said, "Please, hurry, Martin. She's talking about some sort of spirit, and she keeps calling your name."

The old man moistened his lips, sent a sidewise glance toward Judy. She came to her feet. "I think you left my coat in the kitchen," she said, although she had no idea where her coat might be, nor did she care. She wanted a word in private with the old caretaker. "Please show me, Martin." She had taken his arm, was almost pushing him out of the room.

Cilla was saying something about "interlopers," and it sounded as though Jimmy Fergussen contradicted her cheerfully. Judy made no effort to catch the words. She drew Martin as far from the door as possible, said in a soft rush, "Martin, Elizabeth saw me on the stairs. She didn't know it was I. She thought it was your spirit. She never believed in it before, but

I think she's afraid that—that maybe you were right, after all."

Martin was hunched over, listening. "But I wasn't right," he said in a husky whisper. "It was—just—you." He shook his head. "It wasn't a spirit."

"It never was." Judy gripped his arm. "There is no such thing as a spirit or ghost, Martin. That man, Hugen, he's been fooling you—and all those others. Taking your money." Martin made no denial, so Judy knew that Martin, too, had paid for ghostly manifestations. "There's no spirit in the lake," Judy went on. "You've got to promise me you'll make Elizabeth understand, once and for all, that you know better now."

The old man nodded. "All right," he said.

"And tell her she saw me on the stairs. Tell her I came out—and you found me. She'll have to believe you."

"I'll tell her," Martin said heavily. He was relinquishing a dream of long standing, a cherished, fantastic dream. "She—she won't make any more noise," he said.

"That's fine." Judy patted his arm. Her eyes went around the room. "Where is my coat, Martin? I didn't see it in there. Is it out here?"

"No. In the bedroom. I'll go and get it."

"Hurry!"

They had to hurry because Cilla was becoming more impatient. Judy heard her coming toward the kitchen. But Martin had retreated out of another door.

Cilla called after him, "Martin! Please hurry. Before the whole house is in an uproar!"

"That whole house was always in an uproar," ran Judy's thought. "That's the kind of a house it is. The kind of people. No, not people. Mostly, it was because of Garth Frazer. And the uproar he caused was not a noisy, boisterous kind, but something underhand, stealthy. A horrible, wild, hateful feeling that made you want to fight against it, when you had no idea how to do so."

But it would be different now. So different. Because Jimmy Fergussen was here. Solid and straight and courageous. Everything that Garth Frazer was not. Jimmy Fergussen would make things come out right, take Freddy away from this place.

Judy drew a deep sigh. It had turned out better than she had ever dreamed, better than having Grace Doyle be the one to decide a course of action. Grace was so far away, too. And Jimmy was right here—ready.

Cilla must be repeating something. Judy heard her say bitingly, "I don't believe you mentioned whom you wished to see in the house?"

Jimmy had come up behind her. He made the answer: "We're calling on Miss Hammond. Calling *for* her, might be a better way to put it."

"Oh?" Cilla said.

"We're Calling on Miss Hammond," Jimmy Said

Judy thought, "Cilla wants Freddy away from the house. She wouldn't stay herself and take care of her own mother, but she resents having Freddy there. She'd be glad if Freddy went away."

Martin came in with Judy's coat over his arm, the little hat dangling rather foolishly from one of his large wrists. He said, "Here, Miss."

He had his own sheep-lined jacket on, a cap pulled over his head. Jimmy took Judy's coat, held it for her. In a few minutes they were walking toward the door which led to the inner stairway. Martin was in the lead. At the door he paused, looked at Cilla.

"This way's the closest," he said. "But the snow's bad by now. Should I shovel a path first?"

"Oh, no!" Judy said. "We don't mind getting a little wet." She turned slightly toward Jimmy. "Do we?" she asked him to agree.

Smiling slightly, he shook his head. They both heard Cilla give a gentle sniff. She was amused at the way the girl gave Martin his orders, but not displeased. Cilla wanted the old man to come as quickly as possible, so that Elizabeth might be quieted—and so she could get her rest.

Cilla never dreamed why Judy and Jimmy Fergussen were in such eager haste to get to the house, to get Freddy away. Or did she know? Was Cilla in the plot against Myrta Mattis, against her own mother? Was she Garth Frazer's accomplice?

They were going down the inner steps. Martin had

a flashlight which danced over the steps. He had turned on a light overhead, not very bright. But Judy could have plainly seen the way she had come before, if her eyes had been focused on the present, Martin, Cilla, herself and Jimmy Fergussen, trailing along, saying nothing. They were all thinking their own thoughts, Judy told herself, and wondered, above all, what were the secrets that Cilla held in her heart.

She could not be planning that horrible business with Garth Frazer, plotting against the life of her own mother. Judy dismissed that. Cilla might be selfish, cold, but she was not guilty of so dreadful a thing. She could not be!

They had come to the garage doors. Martin opened the first one. He turned to them, grouped at his back. "Better button up good," he advised. "The wind's let down. But it's cold. And the snow's deep."

"Oh, we're all right!" Cilla said impatiently.

Martin sighed. "Well," he said, "follow me." And they went out into the cold. Their feet sank into the snow, and walking was anything but easy. Judy felt Jimmy's hand on her arm, a firm, reassuring pressure. Martin had turned toward Cilla, to ask her if she required any help. She told him no in such a way that he stalked on, making each step he took as even as possible, narrow-spaced—so that the others, following, could use the same imprint in lieu of a path.

The wind had died down. But it was still, cold, and dark. Except where a streamer of light ran out along the snow, not far from the way they were going. Judy glanced up once and saw that the beam came from the second floor, where the structure jutted out. She guessed it might be the porch, or Garth Frazer's room. But it was the back of the house. So, perhaps, everyone was still awake.

She decided, dully, that it did not matter, because the cold did not have a reviving effect. Judy felt the waves of weariness almost engulfing her. If it had not been for Jimmy's arm, she might not have cared whether or not they returned to the Mattis house. And it came again, that sensation of unreality. It was incredible that she was here, trudging through the snow in the middle of the night, among people who meant nothing to her.

Oh, but they did mean something. The face of Frederica Hammond came to Judy's mind. The blond girl had said she wished that she, and not Judy, might be the one to make the break from the house. Yes, Freddy meant something. And Myrta Mattis. And poor old Elizabeth, and Martin, too. In this short while, they had taken the threads of Judy's life and woven them tightly with their own.

So that she was here, at the back door of the Mattis house, stamping the snow from her shoes, achingly tired.

She heard Jimmy say, "Someone's in the kitchen. We'll be in shortly. You cold?"

"Not—very."

"Good girl. We'll be out of this in a little while. We can all walk back to my car."

"Oh,—yes!" Judy said.

But the little whispered conversation had given her the prop she needed. It had lighted the spark of hope, so that the weariness and the discomfort of the moment were blotted away. They would get Freddy, go back to Jimmy's car. In a short while she would be back in the city, in her hotel. Judy thought of her own furry slippers. No, the bed, her big wonderful bed. She would sleep and sleep and sleep.

But not yet, not for a while. Not for quite a while.

Cilla had opened the back door and had gone in. Martin stepped aside so that Judy and Jimmy could precede him. Judy heard Cilla cry, "Why, Elizabeth! What are you doing here?"

The woman was standing with her back to the tile sink, as though seeking protection or trying to bolster up her strength. She looked like a person who had seen a ghost and had not been able to forget it.

"I—I couldn't wait up there." She motioned with her head to the stairs. "You said you'd get Martin and hurry back. So I waited here." Her eyes scrutinized Judy, paused. The old woman, Judy knew, was puzzling over her appearance here in the kitchen. But she said nothing, gave no sign. Jimmy Fergussen might have been someone she knew well, for the old eyes dismissed him also. It was Martin she sought. Finding him, her quest was ended.

"You're here, Martin," she said, and Judy saw how her hands were trembling. "I'll go back with you."

Martin came to her awkwardly. "You won't need to be afraid any more, Bess," he said huskily, placing a hand on her arm. "It's—it's all right. It wasn't what you thought. I can explain it to you."

The old woman looked searchingly into his face.

Martin said again, "It's all right. What you said was true. It never was"—his voice lowered to a whisper, but Judy heard—"a spirit."

She knew that he spoke the truth, that he was through believing in his "spirit," and that he was promising her a reasonable explanation of the figure she had seen. At his words Elizabeth underwent a change. A great relief softened her wrinkled face. The strain went out of her hands, clasping and unclasping.

"I'll get my coat, Martin," she said. "You wait. I'll get my coat."

It was on a hook back of a pantry door. Elizabeth hung it over her shoulders, but Martin saw that she put it on, helped her. Then the two of them went out. The door closed.

It was a part of the strangeness that they should stand here, Judy and Jimmy, while the two old people made their peace and their exit. Cilla had moved a little to one side, nearer to the stove.

Jimmy said to her, "Do you want to tell Freddy we're here?"

Before she could answer, they all heard footsteps on the stairs, coming down from the upper hallway.

It was Garth Frazer, fully clothed, who appeared first. Harris, also dressed, came after him, stood behind him on the stairs leading to the kitchen.

He said, "Cilla?" and stopped, looking down over them. His eyes came back to Judy's face. It seemed that he recognized her, that he was about to say her name, when Jimmy stepped forward and took the initiative.

"This is Miss Garland," he said. "I'm Captain Fergussen. We're friends of Freddy Hammond's."

Cilla put a hand over her mouth. "They told me the same thing," she said. "When I went out to the garage to get Martin, I found them there, having tea with him." She yawned openly. "You talk to them, Garth. I'm deathly tired."

Cilla wanted them to go, that was certain. And she wanted Freddy to leave the house. But perhaps she thought there might be an awkward scene, something to interfere with her comfort. She had removed Elizabeth and her wailing, and she must believe that Garth Frazer was quite capable of dismissing these last two arrivals.

So Cilla went up the stairs, and there were now four of them left in the tiled kitchen: Judy and Jimmy, Garth and Harris.

It was a kind of game. You were the pawn. You were pushed this way and that way. You were blocked. Someone jumped. Someone was put out of the game. And then you were pushed again.

Garth Frazer said to Jimmy, "It's late. I'm afraid Miss Hammond is asleep."

Jimmy said, grimly, "I'd appreciate it if you told her we are here."

Garth Frazer was smiling. What it meant, Judy could not guess. He motioned up the short flight. "If you will follow me," he said, and it was more of a command than an invitation.

Judy had seen only the side of his face before, his neck, the graying hair pressed close to his head. But he looked as she had thought he would look. Deep-set eyes, long upper lip, not unhandsome. A face that would fool most people—because most people would trust him.

"But I know better," Judy thought. "He can't fool me! Nor Jimmy. We'll get Freddy out of here. They can't stop us!"

Garth was leading the way to the living-room, which Judy had seen only vaguely those long hours ago, when she had fled the roundabout way from the stairs to the kitchen.

Garth walked ahead. She and Jimmy followed. Harris came last. Once, as they moved along, Judy paused and turned to look at Jimmy Fergussen. She knew that he shared her thought, with grim determination: Together, they would get Freddy out of here!

CHAPTER TWELVE

APPRECIATIVE AUDIENCE

Garth Frazer motioned the two of them to be seated, on the davenport which Judy had gripped before, which had kept her from falling. It seemed that she almost fell into its depths now. She had a vague wish to put her head down on the rounded arm, to close her eyes.

But that could not be—not until everything had been straightened out, until Freddy had been released. That was what she must think about—that, and nothing more: getting Freddy away from here.

Jimmy was sitting next to her, on the edge of the couch. Across from them was Garth Frazer in a deep chair. Harris stood back a little, near the archway that gave into the dining-room.

A smile twisted Frazer's mouth. He looked lightly over Jimmy's brown overcoat and what showed of his business suit. "Captain Fergussen?" he said.

Judy saw Jimmy flush. "Was," Jimmy said shortly. "And will be again. This is a short intermission. I forget, now and then, that I'm a civilian."

Frazer nodded. It seemed with approval. He looked at Judy.

"You'll have to forgive my niece," he said. "She's

very tired, Miss Garland." Now his eyes rested on both of them. "And having the two of you dropping in at this hour," he broke off, shrugging lightly, "well, it is—unusual."

Unusual, thought Judy, was far from what it was. It was *incredible. Impossible.* But here they were, nonetheless. She and Jimmy.

And here, she reminded herself, was Garth Frazer. The man who was at the bottom of all the hateful strangeness, the man who held Freddy a prisoner. He might appear to know them and welcome them, but Judy meant to cling to what she knew to be facts.

She heard Jimmy saying, "We've had quite a time, getting here. And we'd like to leave as soon as possible. I'm sure Freddy would prefer to know that we're here, and go back with us."

Garth Frazer's eyes went toward a great window that led onto the lake, and back again. "It *is* a bad night," he admitted. "But, if you could wait until the morning," he broke off. "My sister has been ill, and Freddy—"

A thin, taut line seemed to snap in Judy's mind at that moment. She was suddenly furious at the poised, smiling man before her. Furious at all of them—they were so desperately determined to be away from the Mattis house that nothing else mattered. She was on her feet before she knew it, glaring defiantly into the face of Garth Frazer, unafraid, the angry words flowing from lips that could not be hers. But they were hers. She heard herself talking.

"You can't keep Freddy here. Not any longer! And you don't need to pretend, Garth Frazer. Because I know! Do you understand, I *know!* I was here—before—when you came into Myrta's room. I heard—everything. And Freddy told me, too! So you'd better let her go. Do you hear? You let Freddy come with us—now!"

Garth Frazer had also risen. Amazement seemed written on his face. But that passed. He said, "I don't believe I quite understand, Miss Garland."

"Oh, yes you do!" Judy flared. "You know how you've been duping Myrta all along, making her think she was sick. Making her want that—that medicine. YOU wouldn't give it to her. But you make her ask for it. You tried to make Freddy give it to her, too!"

Someone had come down the steps. Judy turned, but saw no one. Only the picture with the dancing pair. She turned back swiftly to Garth Frazer. His face was working queerly. He looked pale.

"Do you—do you realize what you're saying?" he asked.

"Of course I know what I'm saying!" Judy went on hotly. She saw Jimmy's hand reaching to her, as though he were going to say something. But he only stood there, his eyes fixed on her face. Jimmy was going to know it all, too. Everything. They would bring this man to justice. "Freddy is a prisoner here," Judy went on. "You wouldn't let her go. Why, you—you even had Elizabeth take her things—and hide them!"

Garth Frazer's lower lip came up, over the long upper lip. His arms crossed over his chest. When Judy paused, there was a small silence. It seemed that Jimmy said, "Is that true, Judy? Is that really the truth?" in a way that said he knew it must be the truth and that he was ready to put his hard fingers around Frazer's neck.

It was Harris who broke out, "Now, now, I wouldn't be too hasty, my girl." Judy looked at him as he came nearer. His square face was all concern, not for Frazer, but, oddly, for herself.

Garth Frazer said, thoughtfully, "How did you happen to come here, Miss Garland?"

"You don't believe me." Judy looked without fear into his face. "You'll have to believe me because I know. You see, I know—all that's going on."

"Yes," the man said, as though to pacify her. "You told me that. But now, about your coming here?"

"I came on the bus. Martin was out in the front of the house, back of one of the urns. He didn't see me get off. He thought I was a—a spirit. He chased me and I ran." She took a deep, quick breath.

Garth Frazer said, "Yes? And then?"

"I came into the kitchen. Elizabeth didn't want me to come in. She was afraid of you." Judy looked him up and down. "Everybody's afraid of you." But the way she said it told him that she was not afraid. To make certain, she said the words: "But I'm not afraid."

Was it a smile that turned his lips upward? "I can see that," he said. "And then—?"

And then what? So much had happened. Judy tried to think, but for a moment a dull murmuring sound grew in her head, made thinking impossible. She felt Jimmy's hand on her arm, heard him say, "Go on, Judy."

"Then—Freddy came down to the kitchen. She took me up to her room. I was in there when you and Cilla and—" she looked at Harris—"and you came in. After you went away, Freddy told me about—everything. I put on one of Myrta's white capes and went down the stairs."

"You were Elizabeth's spirit," Garth Frazer said. "She did see something."

"Yes, she saw me. But I got away—through here." Her eyes went about the room. "And then down to the torture room."

Jimmy exploded, "The torture room!"

"That's what they called it," Judy told him. "It's a place you get to under the kitchen steps. Cilla called it the torture room when she was little—and being mean to Freddy." It *sounded* little, and very young, even to Judy's ears. And she felt as helpless as a child. Because, looking at Garth Frazer, she did not see the man cringe before her. He stood stolidly, a frown creasing his forehead, one hand rubbing his chin. He was like a rock, against which her torrent of words had splashed harmlessly. She turned to Jimmy Fergussen. "You believe me, don't you, Jimmy?"

"You bet I do!" he gritted. "And I think it's about—!"

"Just a moment," Garth Frazer begged quietly. Jimmy, too, felt that though Judy spoke the truth, the man had some explanation to give, one that rated attention. Jimmy said, "Make it quick!"

"I'll try to," Garth Frazer said, and he looked at Judy. "How did you happen to come here in the first place, Miss Garland?" he asked. "Had you known Frederica—before?"

Judy told him the truth. "No, I never saw her until today. I was in Dora Brit's costume shop. There was a beautiful gown there that Freddy had hidden in one of the cabinets. Mrs. Brit wanted me to return it. So I looked Freddy up. I went to her apartment. It's in the Doyles' house. They—they were worried about Freddy. They asked me to come here and see her—and find out what was the matter."

She was spent. Had there been more to tell, her strength did not last long enough to let her say it. She murmured—it was almost a sob—"That's—all."

Jimmy fumed, "And it's enough. What difference does it make to you why Judy came here? Or why I did? It's our business and Freddy's, and you'd better get her down here—or I will!"

"Please," Garth Frazer said, "if you'll just sit down." He motioned to the davenport behind them. "You see, it *is* my business. Which Freddy—and Miss Garland—have greatly misunderstood."

A certain quality in his tone made them listen, made them sink back on the couch. Harris Morley had been pacing about behind Garth Frazer. In the quiet that fell upon them, his cough seemed mountainous.

Garth Frazer said, "You, too, Harris, though most of this is over your head."

Ill at ease, Harris took a chair farther away. Garth Frazer sat as he had before, facing Judy and Jimmy. His hand took out a white pencil which he rolled in his fingers, seeking a beginning. He found it presently. "In the first place," he said slowly, "there is nothing the matter with Myrta except—" he paused briefly—"too many unappreciative audiences. And some unfavorable publicity." He looked directly at Judy. "You knew she sang?"

Judy said, "Yes. I recognized her—Lucia Grayson." The thought took her, for a happy moment, away from the room. "She sings beautifully. I've admired her for a long time. I have so many of her recordings."

Garth Frazer looked at her with deep approval. He said, "Yes, a magnificent voice. And"—he drew a long breath—"and the wrong kind of pride to back it up." He seemed to be talking away from them, more as though he were thinking aloud to himself. "When trouble came, Myrta took refuge in flight. To be exact, in bed—in sickness. This was a habit of long standing. Many times, I had been able to argue her out of the idea. But this time I did not succeed. It was no use.

If Myrta couldn't get praise, she would take pity."

Judy murmured, "I didn't know she'd been ill."

Garth Frazer said, "She only informed those closely associated with her. But remember, Myrta has not been ill, other than suffering from a case of wounded pride." He moved the pencil to the other hand, looked at it thoughtfully. "And so," he said, "the pills."

Judy gave a start.

Garth Frazer went on, "The nice little sugar candy pills. I got them out of a play nurse kit belonging to the daughter of a friend of mine."

It seemed unbelievable, and yet it was true. Judy was sure it was the truth. She murmured weakly, "They were—just—candy?"

"That's all." He was smiling, a twisted sad kind of smile, and leaned back in his chair. "And so," he went on, "we come to Freddy. I called to ask her out here. I was grateful that Myrta liked having her around. Myrta loves to be pampered, and Frederica did a marvelous job of it."

Judy could only stare at him. The way he spoke of Freddy he seemed genuinely fond of the girl. Of Myrta, too. "Perhaps," Judy thought, "I'm too tired to understand what he's saying." But she knew that she was not too tired. It was only that things had taken on a different light. Like the sky with the first streaks of dawn—it is the same sky, but the little streaks change it completely, and bring a promise of the coming day.

Garth Frazer Tried to Explain the Situation

That was what Judy felt, over and above the weight of weariness—the promise of something good to come. She leaned forward, waiting for Garth Frazer to speak. She knew that he had Jimmy's full attention also, and that Jimmy's attitude had also undergone a change.

Garth Frazer looked straight at the girl. "About that costume," he said slowly, "that white gown."

Judy took a deep breath. The *white gown*. The *hoodoo costume* that had brought her into this whole strange adventure.

"Myrta sent Freddy in with that. And I was, well, worried. I thought it was a last-minute generosity before giving up the will to live." He was looking over her head again, thinking back. "So I kept Freddy on. I even had Elizabeth take away her things because I didn't want her to leave. She had a way of reaching Myrta"—he seemed to have some difficulty swallowing—"a glowing spirit of gentleness and generosity. And I tried to get her to push the pills down Myrta." The smile twitched about his mouth. "The candy drops," he corrected.

Jimmy spoke up. "You were going to make Freddy stay on here?"

"For a time," Garth Frazer admitted. "But taking her clothes wouldn't have stopped Freddy, if she had really wanted to go. That wouldn't have held her. She loves Myrta, and Myrta's genuinely fond of her."

From the stairway, there came the sound of a sob,

a choking, pathetic sound. Garth Frazer seemed to be lifted out of his chair. Judy and Jimmy rose hastily, turned in the direction of the landing.

Garth Frazer said, "Myrta! Myrta, is that you?"

From higher above their heads, a clear young voice called, "Aunt Myrta! Oh, are you all right?" Judy recognized the voice—it was Freddy who came flying down the stairs, to the landing.

Garth Frazer and Jimmy went together to where the two were locked in each other's arms. Myrta was sobbing, "Freddy! Oh, my dear little girl." And Frederica soothed, "Don't cry, Aunt Myrta. Please don't. It's all right."

There was a gentle confusion, bringing them down into the living-room. A golden moment dawned for Freddy when Jimmy Fergussen crushed her in his arms.

Quiet came, after a time, with Myrta and Freddy joining the circle. Judy saw that Myrta wore the robe Freddy had longed to see her wear, and that, despite her recent tears, the woman had never looked more beautiful. Garth accused her, gently, of eavesdropping, and Myrta straightway admitted her guilt.

"That time, I heard exactly what I needed to hear," she said. "What you should have told me long ago, Garth."

"I tried to," he said. "But—"

"But I wouldn't listen. I had to crawl away and hide—and lick my wounds." She looked over to where

Freddy sat next to Jimmy, their fingers interlocked. "No," she amended, "it was Freddy who had to pamper me."

"I didn't have to," Freddy corrected. "I—I wanted to be with you, Aunt Myrta, but I didn't know. I—I thought—" she broke off, looked quickly at Garth Frazer, who took up her thought:

"That I was planning to poison Myrta. Cunningly." He shook his head. "I was clumsy. Overdid my part. I'm no actor, I'll admit. But, if you knew the way things stand, Freddy, you'd never accuse me of wanting to get Myrta out of the way." He looked at the lovely woman and they exchanged a smile of understanding.

Freddy said, "What do you mean?"

"I did not have," Garth said slowly, "what every reasonable detective looks for—a motive. There was no way I could profit by—"

"By my death," Myrta added, in a most lively manner. "I think what Garth is trying to say is that I'm careless. I've been a spender. I know he'll take care of me, if I get in desperate straits, and so I never worry enough to take care of myself."

Garth said, "It's not that bad, Myrta."

"Oh, yes it is," she said. "I've been a parasite. A kind of nasty one."

Garth Frazer smiled at her. He turned again to Freddy, "About your staying here, my dear," he went on mildly, "I had no intention of keeping you much longer. There is that job of yours—at Maley's."

Freddy's eyes came wide open. "How did you know about that?" she said.

Myrta told her. "Garth owns the store, my dear. I don't believe I told you."

"You—*own it!*" Freddy stared at him. "Then—you mean—?"

"Yes, I got you the job, Freddy. I've been watching your work for some time. I—I felt that we had neglected you, Myrta and I."

"I did the neglecting," Myrta said hotly. "You were only a man, an uncle, Garth. But Freddy's mother and I were sisters—I should never have let her go away to school when she was so little. I should have kept her here, close to me."

Jimmy got a word in edgewise. "I think Freddy's done pretty well. A credit to all of you." He grinned at Garth Frazer. "And you might not have that artist in your advertising department for any length of time."

The older man nodded. "That's all right. But the job's there, any time she wants it."

From above them, in the little silence that settled, came Cilla's voice, which was, and was not, as cool and aloof as Judy knew it:

"Don't you think it's about time to bring the family session to a close? You'd better get to bed, mother."

Judy thought, through the maze that was no longer one of fear, of things warped and misunderstood, that perhaps Cilla had heard some things here this night that had been good for her, too.

Myrta came to her feet. "I'll be right up, darling," she said, and turned to Garth. "I'm starting to practice again tomorrow." Judy was looking at her warmly, with a depth of adulation. When Myrta came to her swiftly, took both her hands and drew the girl to her feet, Judy felt suddenly and woefully lost. "It is to you, my dear," she said, "that we owe a tremendous vote of thanks."

"Why," Judy gasped, "I didn't do a thing!"

Someone laughed, and the laugh grew—relief after the tension.

Judy insisted, "It was Freddy, really. Freddy is the one."

"I know what Freddy has done," Myrta Mattis said fondly. "And I mean to show my gratitude. But I know what you did, too, Judy." She bent and kissed the girl's cheek. "What a horrible night you must have had."

"But it wasn't—" Judy started to protest, because, strangely, the night did not seem horrible. Not now, when it was over. And the day would be shining through—for all of them.

From above, Cilla called again, "Mother, are you coming?"

"Right away, dear," Myrta promised. And she spoke of how they all had suffered. "It's not so hard on me," she reminded them. "I've been in bed so much, I feel as though I'd like to walk around the lake right now!"

Protests rose, and over them Jimmy remembered his car.

"Can you get it out, and come back?" Myrta asked him. "We could have a family gathering. Really." She beamed approval at him, standing beside her. "A kind of engagement party?"

Jimmy said, "I'll be back."

Myrta moved toward the stairs, but paused before reaching the landing. She said, "Judy, where is that white gown now?"

Where *was* it?

Freddy said, "It's still wrapped up, the way you brought it out."

"Unwrap it, will you?" Myrta asked gently. "I—I'd like you to keep it, Judy—if you want to. As a kind of remembrance. And to keep you reminded of—my gratitude."

Myrta Mattis must have felt it then—the glow that came from the hearts of them, her wholly appreciative audience.

"I'd love to have it," Judy said.

Still Myrta hesitated. "It would be nice—if you could stay long enough to get rested up a little. And then put it on for me, for us. Would you?"

Judy thought of her waylaid plans, of the time she had lost. But could the time be called lost when so much good, so much happiness had resulted? She said, "I'll stay, and I'll love putting it on."

Harris Morley had sat in the background, fondling his cold pipe. No one had paid especial attention to him, but it was presently evident that he had missed nothing of what was going on. He spoke suddenly, like a happy gust of wind. "The way I remember that dress, I'd say the girl would be a knockout in it!"

WHITMAN
AUTHORIZED EDITIONS

SYLVIA SANDERS and the Tangled Web
PATTY O'NEAL on the Airways
LONG RIDER and the Treasure of Vanished Men
BOY SAILOR with John Paul Jones
BOY FIGHTER with Andrew Jackson
GINGER ROGERS and the Riddle of the Scarlet Cloak
SHIRLEY TEMPLE and the Spirit of Dragonwood
SHIRLEY TEMPLE and the Screaming Specter
ROY ROGERS and the Gopher Creek Gunman
ROY ROGERS and the Raiders of Sawtooth Ridge
GENE AUTRY and the Thief River Outlaws
GENE AUTRY and the Redwood Pirates
RED RYDER and the Mystery of the Whispering Walls
RED RYDER and the Secret of Wolf Canyon
RED RYDER and the Adventure at Chimney Rock
SANDRA of the Girl Orchestra
PEGGY PARKER, Girl Inventor
DON WINSLOW and the Scorpion's Stronghold
KING OF THE ROYAL MOUNTED and the Ghost Guns of Roaring River
WINNIE WINKLE and the Diamond Heirlooms
BETTY HUTTON and the Romance of Palmetto Island
QUIZ KIDS and the Crazy Question Mystery

The books listed above may be purchased at the same store where you secured this book.

Lightning Source UK Ltd.
Milton Keynes UK
UKHW011947120819
347845UK00001B/105/P

9 781479 440733